# OPERATION CHARIOT

## by

## Duncan Harding

**THUNDERCHILD PUBLISHING**
Huntsville, Alabama

**OPERATION CHARIOT**

Published by arrangement with the Charles Whiting literary estate.

ISBN-13: 978-1979944120
ISBN-10: 1979944121

Published by Thunderchild Publishing.  Find us at
https://ourworlds.net/thunderchild_cms/

# The Prelude

# ONE

Hitler made his summing up, while the generals and admirals listened attentively. "From past experience, I do not believe the British are capable of making and carrying out lightning decisions. They are incapable of transferring their bomber and fighter aircraft to south-east England for an attack on our ships in the Dover Straits, with the speed that the Naval Staff and Vice-Admiral Ciliax predict."

The Führer sighed wearily, as if exhausted by his efforts to instil his own boldness into his senior officers.

"Picture what would happen if the situation were reversed," he went on, trying to fire them to some enthusiasm, "and a surprise report came in that British battleships had appeared in the Thames estuary and were heading for the Straits of Dover. Even *we* could scarcely bring up our aircraft swiftly and methodically.

The situation of the Brest Group is like that of a patient with cancer who is doomed unless he submits to an operation. An operation, which though it may have to be drastic, will at least offer some hope of saving the patient's life. The passage of our ships through the Channel is such an operation. It must be attempted."

Hitler's voice rose, filled abruptly with that thick Austrian fervour which had once roused the brown-shirted mob at Nuremburg to frenzied hysteria in the old days before the war. "There is nothing to be gained by leaving our ships at Brest. Their flypaper effect — that of tying up enemy air forces — may not continue for long. Only as long as the ships remain in battleworthy condition will the enemy feel obliged to attack.

But the moment they are seriously damaged — and that could happen any day — the enemy will discontinue his attacks, and thereby nullify the one and only advantage derived from leaving our ships at Brest."

Hitler stared directly at Vice-Admiral Ciliax, the tall, middle-aged sailor who was to command the operation. *"Herr Admiral,* on the eleventh of February, you will take the *Scharnhorst, Gneisenau* and the *Prinz Eugen* out of Brest and proceed at full speed up the English Channel to Kiel. Clear?"

*"Klar, mein Führer!"* Ciliax clicked stiffly to attention.

"Good." Hitler smiled suddenly, complete master of the situation, now he had convinced the assembled officers of the planning staff to accept his bold venture against their better judgement. "And gentlemen, I can tell you this. I'd be willing to pay one thousand gold marks to see the look on that drunken old Jewish sot, Churchill's face when he learns just how we have tricked him at Brest ..."

# TWO

At six o'clock the flotilla of E-boats came hissing across the green, dark sea from Cherbourg, bows high out of the water, twin white trails of wild spray floating behind them like wings. Careening round in a great crazy circle, the flotilla split into two, taking up their positions on the far side of the protective screen formed by the destroyers.

Admiral Ciliax on the *Scharnhorst* nodded his approval. Everything was working according to plan. His escape force now totalled twenty-five ships, and already he could see the first dark specks on the dirty white horizon to the east, which indicated that his air cover was beginning to arrive from their French fields. Hitler's gamble looked as if it might pay off after all.

He turned to his second-in-command. "When the fighters arrive," he ordered, "signal them to fly just above the water. I don't want the British radar to start picking them up at this stage of the operation."

"*Jawohl, Herr Admiral.* I'll see to it personally." He turned to the waiting signaller. The fleet had been on radio silence ever since the ships had left Brest six hours before.

"Stand-by to send message, *Obermaat!*" he barked.

The petty officer tensed over his signal lamp.

An hour passed. And another. The escape fleet ran into a new minefield off Dieppe. Four minesweepers hurried out from the French harbour and did a quick sweep. Ciliax took a chance. He ordered the capital ships to pass through the hastily swept path first. Nothing happened. The minesweepers had done their job well.

At eleven o'clock precisely, Admiral Ciliax received his first bit of bad news since "Operation Cerberus" had started. A young signals lieutenant rattled up the gangway to the *Scharnhorst's* bridge, flimsy in his hand, and in his haste forgot to salute. *"Herr Admiral —"* he began.

"First, salute!" Ciliax interrupted him. In thirty years of naval service he had never allowed anything to interfere with the courtesies of military duty.

The boy flushed and saluted.

Ciliax smiled. "Well?"

"Intercept, sir." The Lieutenant almost thrust the flimsy at him, as if it were red-hot.

*"Damn, damn, damn!"* Ciliax cursed.

"What is it, sir?" his second-in-command asked anxiously.

"The Tommies have spotted us. Fighter. Reports three capital ships and twenty other ships steaming at high speed for the Straits of Dover: Position fifty miles off the mouth of the Somme."

"Ach, heaven, arse and twine!" his second-in-command cursed too, his face suddenly very pale. "That's splendid. *Jetzt gib is Krach and Wonne!"*

The secret was out,


The Wellingtons, the Spitfires and the ancient naval Swordfishes attacked again and again. But as Hitler had predicted, they had been thrown into the air too hastily and their attack on the fleet steaming steadily northwards, was totally without plan.

The Me-109s and Focke-Wulf 190s, on the other hand, had their every move planned. Under the command of Colonel Adolf Galland, directing the defence from an Me-110 sitting out of range, the German fighters climbed parallel to the attack force as they were coming up on a swift lift. Then they came in at 400 mph, yellow noses spinning crazily, the frontal attacks hitting the low squadrons, the rear attacks going for the high and lead squadrons.

Wellingtons began to fall out of the grey overcast sky like black leaves, great pieces of aluminium dropping off them, emergency doors, wings, prematurely opened parachutes streaming by the survivors, as they ploughed on grimly to their targets.

The Focke-Wulfs took over. Lowering their undercarriages and tilting up their yellow-painted noses to lower their speed, they attempted deflection fire from five hundred metres' range, while the Me-109s massed to come in for the second attack.

The fighters hissed above the shattered British squadrons, their pilots cursing the ice which at that height, was beginning to form on their cockpits and blind them, and released their little parachute bombs. Almost immediately the small stick bombs began to explode among the British planes. A Wellington disintegrated in mid-air. When the smoke vanished, there was nothing there. Another slipped to port then streamed out of the grey sky, trailing fiery scarlet flame behind it. It hurtled straight into the sea and disappeared in a great white flurry of water. More and more followed. But still the British pressed home their furious attack.

At three o'clock, off the Belgian coast, with the fleet, all guns chattering wildly now, the cumbersome twin-winged Swordfishes from the British Fleet Air Arm began dropping mines ahead of the German ships.

Thirty minutes later Admiral Ciliax's flagship the *Scharnhorst,* all twenty-six thousand tons of her, was shaken by a violent explosion. Suddenly all her lights went out and her radio fell silent.

Ciliax grabbed hold of the rail on the bridge just in time and cried in fury. *"Scheisse — eine Mine!"* Trailing a thick film of oil behind her, the *Scharnhorst,* slowly but inevitably, came to a halt.

For a moment Ciliax hesitated. It went against the grain to abandon the battleship, the pride of the German Navy. Yet there were twenty-other odd ships under his command, including the *Gneisenau* and *Prinz Eugen.* They came first, not the outdated naval tradition of the captain going down with his ship.

"All right," he yelled to his second-in-command above the roar of the British bombers, who were now concentrating their attack on the stricken *Scharnhorst,* "order the *Z.29* to come alongside. She can take me and the command staff off." Ciliax stared up at the sky. The weather was beginning to deteriorate rapidly. Visibility was down to two kilometres and the cloud ceiling couldn't be more than two hundred metres. Any minute now, it would begin to rain. With a bit of luck, the *Scharnhorst's* skipper might be able to get the stricken ship underway, and escape before the Tommies could launch an all-out attack on the battleship.

Five minutes later, Admiral Ciliax was being winched across the heaving green waves in a bosun's chair, to the waiting destroyer, leaving the *Scharnhorst* to her fate.


*"Object ahead, skipper!"* HMS *Rose's* first officer, Lieutenant Doan sang out, in that easy American way of his. "Straight ahead. About four miles off."

Lieutenant-Commander John Lamb, the *Rose's* captain, swung up his binoculars hastily, bracing his feet against the destroyer's wildly heaving deck. A long sleek grey object slipped into the white gleaming circle of the lenses. He recognized it immediately. But for a moment something — perhaps it was fear — stopped him from saying the ship's name aloud. Then he pulled himself together. "It's the *Scharnhorst,"* he announced almost calmly. "All twenty-six thousand tons and nine 11-inch guns of her."

"Oh, my aching back!" Doan groaned. "What good are our five-inch pop-guns against that kind of artillery?"

Commander Lamb forced a smile he didn't feel. "I don't know, Doan, but we'll soon find out, won't we?" He swung round to the grizzled, monkey-faced petty officer who had already taken over the wheel from the pale, frightened rating, and was ready for action. "Cox'n, sound action stations!"

Chief Petty Officer Horst Degenhardt didn't hesitate. He hit the button. In a flash the whole ship was alarmed. With the bells clanging their stomach-turning frenzied call to "action stations", cursing, sliding, frightened seamen, scrambling into their flash-gear and steel helmets, ran across the slick icy deck to their stations. Below, the ER.9 gave the destroyer all the speed her 30,000 hp engines could produce. Abruptly the *Rose* was hitting each new wave, as if it was made of solid brick.

On the bridge, indifferent to the drenching spray, the officers watched as the great grey ship loomed up larger and larger on the horizon, suddenly it seemed to fill it, in all its frightening menace.

The *Scharnhorst* spotted them. Abruptly the length of her port bow rippled with dazzling lights. In an instant a grey wall of flying spray rose fifty feet in the air before the destroyer. The *Rose* trembled madly.

Lamb grabbed for the speaking tube. "Stand by for torpedo attack, Sub!" he rapped.

Down below, the frightened 18-year-old sub-lieutenant lick his dry lips and said: "Ay, ay, sir!" Hastily he bent his head over the three-pronged sight, his finger on the torpedo-firing button, his skinny bottom sticking up absurdly in the air.

Now the *Rose's* forward five-inch guns were hammering away. Lamb could see their shells dropping just short of the great ship. Still, he told himself, even if they had struck the *Scharnhorst,* they would have done about as much damage as a tennis ball. The German battleship's armour was metre-thick. The *Rose's* only hope was to get in to about two thousand yards range and let the German have a salvo of torpedoes under the waterline.

But that wasn't the way it happened.

Just as the tossing, twisting destroyer had almost closed to torpedo range, the *Scharnhorst* stopped firing. One moment every gun on the battleship's port side was hammering away at the little — overage destroyer; the next, they were all silent. An instant later, Commander Lamb saw the reason why.

A squadron of Messerschmitt 109s — nine of them — were hurtling through the grey smoke, line abreast, machine guns already chattering redly, heading straight for HMS *Rose.*

Immediately the destroyer's anti-aircraft guns took up the new challenge. At the "Chicago pianos" — the banked, multiple pom-poms — the gunners already sweating in spite of the intense cold, swung back and forth desperately, peppering the sky to the *Rose's* front with half-inch shells.

A fighter stopped suddenly in mid-air. The white blob of the pilot's face disappeared abruptly behind a spider's web of splintered perspex. For one long moment the plane seemed to hang there, then suddenly it fell out of the sky, trailing al long red flame behind it. The pilot did not escape. Another Messerschmitt was hit and side-slipped to the side. But the other seven kept on coming.

In an instant they had swamped the *Rose* with their fire. Their 20 mm cannon shells tore up the wooden deck. A burst ripped across the bridge. Glass splintered. A stream of vicious blue sparks danced towards the young rating whom Degenhardt had relieved at the wheel. He ducked. Too late! The shells gouged the eyes out of him, turning his face into a bloody red pulp. He fell screaming, the deck at his feet a sudden wet scarlet.

The Messerschmitts roared over the *Rose,* dragging their evil black shadows behind them, scything the heeling, swaying destroyer with their deadly shells. Men went down everywhere. A "Chicago piano" exploded in a great crash of dark orange. Commander Lamb caught a glimpse of the gunner, still strapped into his seat, but minus his head, sailing through the burning air. He grabbed the tube and yelled fervently. "Engine-room, for Chrissake, make smoke ... *make smoke!"*

As the thick white choking smoke started to issue from the funnel, Petty Officer Degenhardt swung the wheel to port, sending the destroyer lurching to one side wildly, her top mast seeming almost to touch the water. A moment later the *Rose* had disappeared into the smoke, safe from the Messerschmitts' relentless fire and heading back the way she had come, leaving the *Scharnhorst* to limp to port and safety.

HMS *Rose's* luck had run out on her once again ...

# THREE

Grimly the old man, with the face of an occidental Buddha who liked the good things of this life, read through the sentence in the *Times* once again, the spectacles resting on the end of his stubby baby's nose. "Vice-Admiral Ciliax has succeeded where the Duke of Medina Sidonia failed ... nothing more mortifying to the pride of sea power has happened in Home Waters since the seventeenth century ..."

"Pah!" the old man crumpled the newspaper with an angry gesture and threw it at the paper-littered floor of his office. "Absolute rubbish!" he cried to no one in particular. "Balderdash!"

But he knew in his heart the anonymous *Times'* leader-writer was justified. The Boche had sailed a fleet of ships, over two dozen of them, right through the Channel — the *English* Channel — and all the might of the Royal Navy and the Royal Air Force had not been able to stop them. No wonder the British public was howling for the blood of the culprits; he was going to have to face a very unpleasant couple of hours in the House this afternoon.

And the people were right. The Boche had been a jump ahead of the Admiralty right from the start of the whole operation. They had done the completely unexpected, taken a huge risk, jammed and fooled British radar, and shown to the whole world that Britain's pride, the Royal Navy, had little ability to improvise when faced with a surprise situation.

Angrily he pressed his buzzer.

"Sir?" his private secretary's voice came through the intercom.

13

"Is he there?" Suddenly the old man realized he had forgotten to put his false teeth in again after lunch. He took them out of the handkerchief, dipped them swiftly in the glass of brandy on the littered desk in front of him and replaced them. He asked once more, but now with the full authority of that great voice of his which had thrilled a nation over the last two black years, "is he there already!"

"Yes, Prime Minister. He's waiting in the ante-room."

"Then send him immediately," Winston Churchill boomed, "there is work to be done."

Commodore First Class, Lord Louis Mountbatten, the new head of Combined Operations, came bounding in with the same energy and determination that had once made him a feared opponent in the pre-war polo fields, among the fashionable set of those carefree days. He gave the old man behind the desk an immaculate naval salute and waited expectantly.

Churchill took his time, sizing up the good-looking officer standing in front of him. He knew Mountbatten's pre-war image had been that of a wealthy playboy: expensive flat in Mayfair, polo, the obligatory attendance at fashionable resorts on the Continent. Yet all the same the "playboy" had proved himself as a destroyer flotilla commander in the Mediterranean, fighting in his last ship, HMS *Kelly,* off Crete, to the end, in the previous year. In spite of his wealth and film-star looks, Churchill knew that here he had the man he wanted: an officer who combined energy, brains and determination.

"Sit down, Mountbatten," he ordered suddenly.

The Commodore sat down, reached instinctively for his silver cigarette case, then thought better of it. He knew of old that Churchill could be offended by the slightest movement if it broke his concentration — and it was obvious that at the moment the Old Man *was* concentrating.

"You read the *Times's* first leader this morning, no doubt, Mountbatten?"

"Yessir. A real stinker," Mountbatten replied, irrepressibly.

"A real stinker indeed!" Churchill agreed glumly. "Not to put too fine a point on it, we've been kicked up the rear in our own backyard and you can imagine what that bloody Nazi, Hitler, is

14

making of it over there. The airways must be full of his boasting this morning. Damn the man, he has been able to cock a snook at the whole might of the great British Navy and get away with it!"

"Yessir," Mountbatten said sympathetically. He knew just how much the Old Man felt for the Senior Service and its tradition. After all, the Navy had been Churchill's first command in 1939 after more than a decade in the political wilderness. "But I doubt if their Lordships will ever allow the Germans to get away with a caper like that again, sir. I'm sure that a few heads are rolling in Signals and Communications this very morning."

"Many," Churchill said darkly. "I've already taken care of that. But what happened in the Channel yesterday is history. We have to think of the future. Mountbatten, what do you know of the German ship, the *Tirpitz?*"

"The *Tirpitz,* sir?" Mountbatten echoed, puzzled by the Old Man's unexpected question. "Why it's the Germans' largest remaining battleship since we sunk her sister ship the *Bismarck* last year."

"That is correct. The *Tirpitz* is probably the biggest ship in the world today with her displacement of 45,000 tons, and her speed makes her faster than all of our capital ships, even the newest, the *Prince of Wales.*"

Mountbatten nodded his agreement.

"Now you know, of course, what a devil of a chase the *Bismarck* led us last May. We had half the damned fleet after her and it cost us the *Hood.* Can you fathom what must be going through that madman Hitler's head after the success of yesterday's Channel operation?"

"You don't mean, sir —"

"I do," Churchill interrupted his excited exclamation. "Intelligence thinks that the *Tirpitz* up there in Norway is preparing for a foray into the Atlantic. Even if he loses her in the venture, he will win with his U-boats. We'll have to take the Home Fleet off convoy duties to go hunting for the *Tirpitz,* and the U-boats will have a field day with our merchant ships. I don't need to tell you, Mountbatten, just how serious our losses are in that area, as it is."

Churchill sighed like a man bearing the cares of the world and stared glumly at the fat grey slugs of the barrage balloons over London, through his window. Suddenly Mountbatten, usually an unemotional man, felt a warm sense of affection for this old, toothless man who had borne the weight of defeat after defeat in these last terrible months. "But sir," he said swiftly, trying to cheer him up, "once the *Tirpitz* is out in the Atlantic, she'll never get back. Their Lordships have learned from the business with the *Bismarck* last year. They'll seal off the Denmark Strait between Greenland and Iceland with subs and aircraft from our carriers. She'll never get back to Norwegian waters."

Churchill snapped out of his gloom. He leaned forward across his big, littered desk and pointed a nicotine-stained forefinger at the younger man almost accusingly. "And that is exactly what Hitler would expect their Lordships do."

"What do you mean, sir?"

"I mean that *Tirpitz* will not attempt to get back to its berth in Norwegian waters."

"But where will she go, sir? There are only a few harbours that can take a ship of that size on the Atlantic seaboard."

With a thick grunt Churchill rose to his feet and jowls shaking angrily, he stumped over to the big wall map, dotted everywhere with little blue and red flags. He stabbed his finger at the coast of France. "That's where she'll head for," he barked. "St Nazaire!"

Mountbatten's mind clicked. Of course! Hadn't the *Bismarck* led the Home Fleet a merry dance of three thousand miles from the Arctic Circle to the Bay of Biscay, with both the British and the German ships almost running out of fuel; Churchill had been forced to order the Home Fleet to keep on going, even if the fuelless battleships had to be towed home to Scapa Flow? And why had she attempted to make the Bay of Biscay? Mountbatten knew the answer instinctively. Because her captain, Admiral Lutjens, had known the only place he could escape the massed attack of the British battleships, was the deep-water port of St Nazaire.

"I can see you are following the train of my thought, Mountbatten," Churchill said and waddled back to his desk. He flopped down in it and busied himself with a cigar while at the back of the other man's mind, an uneasy premonition began to grow, concerning the reason for this surprise summons to Churchill's office this dull, overcast February morning.

Finished with his preparations, Churchill stuck the big Havana between his lips and after lighting it puffed furiously at the cigar, wreathing his pudgy, baby-face in blue smoke before he finally succeeded in getting it going. He breathed a furious stream of smoke and said, "Mountbatten, at this stage of the war, I cannot afford to have the *Tirpitz* coming out of Norwegian waters and attempting to make a run for it. Whatever the outcome, we would lose — to both the U-boats and our new American allies. They certainly would not be impressed by the Navy of their cousins-across-the-sea, especially if their Lordships made as big a hash of it as they did yesterday in Home Waters. In short, Mountbatten, I must discourage the Germans from even attempting to send the *Tirpitz* out."

"And that is why I'm here, sir?"

"Correct. If the German ship has no port to run for, it is my guess she won't make the attempt in the first place. Even that madman Hitler must give his ship's crew a chance of survival."

"Yes, of course, sir. So —"

"So, my dear Mountbatten," Churchill interrupted him once again, "I want your commando chaps to destroy the port of St Nazaire so that there is nowhere along the Atlantic coast which could harbour the *Tirpitz.*"

"I see, sir," Mountbatten answered woodenly, as if he had just confirmed the state of the weather, but his mind was racing wildly. "And when do you expect Combined Operations to carry out the mission, sir?"

Churchill looked up at him gravely, knowing as he always did on such occasions that the words he would now say would condemn some men to death and others to prolonged suffering. "Without delay," he growled. *"St Nazaire must cease to exist as a deep water port by the end of next month, Mountbatten ..."*

# The Plan

# ONE

They were auctioning off the personal effects of the *Rose's* dead in the drill hall when the drafting notices started to go up. Eagerly the "Hostilities Only" men, young fresh-faced 18 and 19 year olds straight from the training schools, crowded around them to find which ships they had been allotted to.

But on this particular bright, March afternoon, those who had had visions of being posted to the comfort of the "battle-wagons", with their cinemas, showers and proper mess-halls were disappointed. The latest draft from Devonport Barracks were all being sent to a destroyer HMS *Rose*.

"What kind of ship is she, Petty Officer?" they asked the hard-faced man in charge of the Drafting Office.

"What kind of ship is she?" he echoed their words with professional joviality. "A fine ship! You've got a good one there, take my word for it. Too good for you HO men in my opinion."

"Why, you served on her, P.O.?" they chorused in unison.

"Not flipping likely," was the petty officer's cheerful reply as he backed into his office to dodge any further questions.

But in Devonport Naval Barracks, like any other naval depot throughout the United Kingdom, there was always some grizzled, ancient "three-striper", prepared to relax over his broom and dig into his fund of naval lore for the price of a *Woodbine* and the promise of a half o' bitter when the pubs opened. The information the draftees wanted about their new posting was not difficult to find out, therefore, and it wasn't very good.

"The *Rose,* eh?" the three-striper said reflectively, tucking his half-smoked, hand-rolled "tickler" carefully behind his left ear and accepting the proffered *Woodbine.* "Ay, I've heard of her all right. More times than you HO rookies have had hot dinners."

"Well?" the eager young faces crowded around the old hand urged. "What's she like?"

"Depends which way you look at it, as the actress said to the Bishop," he replied, taking his time, enjoying the look of frustration in his listeners" eyes. "Some say she's a good ship — and some tell the truth. Yer see, lads, yer can get yersen a medal on her real quick. She did pretty good at Narvik* and last year, too with the commandos at Vaagso."

"Was she at the Vaagso landing?" they asked eagerly.

The old hand seemed not to hear their question. "On the other hand, though, lads, yer can get yersen killed pretty nifty like on the old *Rose —"*

"What yer mean, yer silly old fart?" a sharp cockney voice cut into the rambling explanation.

The old hand turned slowly.

A tall blond sailor stood there, the very epitome of the spiv sailor in his skin-tight suit with enormous bell-bottoms, that certainly weren't regulation, the cuffs of his jumper turned back to reveal the full glory of his large, chromium-plated wrist-watch.

"Are you addressing me, you no-badge AB?" the old hand asked, his face contorted with scorn.

"Of course, I am," Wide Boy Stevens snorted. "Do yer think I talk to myself like you do, you old fart, when you've had a sniff at the barmaid's apron down in the pubs."

Around him the draftees giggled. They all knew Wide Boy. In spite of the fact he wasn't a day older than 19, the exbarrowboy and black-marketeer had a reputation in the "Guz"** for being scared of nothing and nobody. Wide Boy always gave as good as he got — and then some.

* *See Flotilla Attack* for further details.
** Devonport Naval Barracks.

"Come on, pee or get off the pot. What's wrong with the *Rose,* eh?" He thrust a green packet of *Woodbines* at the old hand. "Here, stick them in yer tiddley suit and tell us, mate."

"She's a jinx ship, that's what she is," the old hand answered, slightly appeased by the bribe. "Always has been and always will be. Ran aground off the China Sea in the twenties. Nearly took over by her crew in the troubles in thirties — when you lot was still wetting yer nappies. And now when she's the only ship in the Home Fleet to get within farting distance of them Jerry ships, the *Scharnhorst* and the other one — can't pronounce the name — she runs into the *Luftwaffe* and loses a third of her crew. Now if you asks me, that's more than bad luck — that's a bloody jinx!"

"Ah yer," Wide Boy said, "but no one *is* asking you, is they, old man?" With that he turned and strode away, as if for him the whole matter was already settled. But in spite of his apparent calm, Wide Boy was disturbed. He wasn't afraid of serving on a destroyer, jinxed or not jinxed, but he had set his sights on a battle-wagon, with its thousands of bored sailors, who might well lose two weeks' pay in a housey-housey game and not think twice about it, and where the galleys offered a rich haul to anyone like Wide Boy Stevens with his contacts with Plymouth's black market. For in spite of his often repeated boast to the other ratings at Devonport Naval Barracks that all he wanted was "a quick, happy life and the chance to make a handsome corpse", the shrewd product of London's East End had other plans for himself. The war, he knew, offered unlimited pickings and Wide Boy Stevens was intent on getting more than his fair share of those pickings. Worried by the problems posed by the sudden new posting, Wide Boy marched up the stone steps to his barrack room and sitting on the neatly stacked blankets on his cot, began to count his money to calm himself.

Able Seaman Stevens was not the only one worried about the new posting that particular March afternoon: Just across the water at Plymouth, Lt-Commander Lamb stared down at the list of the new ship's company which Lt. Doan had just handed him, his young face creased in a deep frown.

Above him on the deck, the dockies were still hammering away, repairing the last of the damage from the Messerschmitt attack, while Leading Seaman "Scouse" MacFadden was singing the traditional dirty ditty about the "maiden who was never satisfied" in his thick nasal Liverpudlian accent. But Lamb heard neither the hammers nor Scouse's account of how the "maiden's" dilemma was solved. His attention was concentrated on the ship's list.

"Doesn't look too good, does it, skipper?" Doan said at last, breaking the heavy silence of the little cabin, whose sole decoration was a picture of the skipper's mother and the flag of the *Braunschweig,* which they had helped to sink off Narvik two years before.

"Good! It looks bloody impossible, Doan. Out of two hundred and sixty odd men for this commission, I've got a hundred HO men, straight from the depots, with not one of them having any sea duty — not to mention active service."

Doan, who had deserted from the American Navy before the USA had entered the war, to volunteer for the Canadian Navy and attached duty with the Royal Navy, shrugged easily. It was an old story now; there were never enough trained men to go round in this third year of war. But the skipper always seemed to take it as a personal affront when he received a batch of rookies. "It's all in the luck of the draw, skipper," he said. "As long as they can breathe, the medics pass 'em fit for seagoing duty."

Lamb looked up at him, as if he were seeing Doan's pleasantly handsome face for the very first time. "I know what you're thinking, Doan," he said. "That I'm a bloody old moaner. But this time it's different from before."

"What do you mean, skipper?"

Lamb crooked a finger at him. "Come on, I'll show you." Together they went on to the deck, littered with the dockies' gear, and stared across the dockyard. From Drake's Island a salt breeze ruffled the Sound and swept across the Floe.

Lamb pointed across the black geometry of cranes and grey hulls at HMS *Campbelltown,* where a group of dockies were still working hard at cutting off the tops of the overage destroyer's twin funnels with their bright red torches, to give them a new sloping angle. "Now what do you make of that, Doan?"

"What am I supposed to make of it, skipper?" Doan answered, puzzled. He stared intently at the old ship which he had once known as the USS *Buchanan* before President Roosevelt had traded it to the British for a hunk of Bermuda on a 99-year lease. "They're giving the old bitch a bit of a face-lift, I guess."

Lamb shook his head in mock dismay. "You haven't been working at your recognition charts, I can see that, Doan," he said. "Don't you recognize the new silhouette, eh?"

"Can't say I do, skipper."

"Well, I'll tell you what she looks like. That ship over there is a dead ringer for the Jerry *Möwe* class torpedo boat, now."

Doan whistled softly through his teeth. "How about that!" he exclaimed.

"And what do you make of the fact that together with the *Campbelltown* and Commander Ryder over there in the *Tynedale,*" — he indicated another destroyer with the black stripe of a flotilla leader on its funnel — "the *Rose* is supposed to make up something called the 10th Anti-Submarine Striking Force? An overage Lease-Lend destroyer, a fast Hunt class ship, the *Tynedale,* and the *Rose,* who isn't exactly the fastest ship afloat. And they're supposed to form an anti-submarine striking force! Doan, it just isn't on, I tell you."

"You mean it's a cover job?" Doan asked, sucking his excellent white teeth thoughtfully.

Lamb nodded.

Over at the forward 5-inch gun turret Scouse was coming to the climax of his ditty, regaling the empty turret with the fact that "at last the Maiden cried, I'm satisfied. But the prick of steel went on and on ..."

"But for what, skipper?" Doan asked, as they went back to Lamb's cabin.

"An op," Lamb slumped into his scuffed leather chair wearily, "another bloody op, Doan, and with one third of the *Rose's* crew never even having had as much as a sniff of gunpowder. Now how does that strike you, Doan?"

"Well below the bloody belt, skipper, well below ..."

# TWO

On the morning of March 5th, 1942, the draft from
Devonport Naval Barracks arrived to file their way through a lower
deck littered with drums of oil and paint, packing cases and air hoses
for the dockies' pneumatic drills. They were accompanied by the
mocking ditty of the old hands:

"We're poor little lambs who have gone astray, baa, baa, baa,
Little black sheep who have lost their way, baa, baa, baa.
Gentlemen matelots, all we are, doomed from here to eternity
God have mercy on such as we —"

"All right, all right," Petty Officer Degenhardt's harsh
Prussian voice cut into the ragged chorus decisively, "enough of that
row. Now get about your duties, you men." The singing died at once.
It didn't do to cross Degenhardt. The old hands returned to their
duties while the Petty Officer faced the ragged line of draftees, their
white kitbags and ditty boxes placed at their feet on the littered,
deck. "Now listen to this you lot," he barked above the dockies'
racket, "before the captain comes down. My name's Degenhardt,
Chief Petty Officer Degenhardt, the *Rose's* Coxswain — and I'm a
bastard!" He ran his dark gimlet eyes down their pale-faced ranks, as
if daring anyone to challenge his statement.

"Now, all of you can hear that I'm a Jerry — or I was till
King George in his wisdom, decided to honour me with British
citizenship." He smiled at them realizing that he must have made the
statement a good dozen times now since he had first joined the *Rose*

in '39. Suddenly he wondered how many of the frightened matelots he had made it to were now dead below the waves, but he quickly dismissed the thought. "So that makes me a double bastard, don't it?" he continued. "A chief and a Jerry in one go, eh?"

"Cor," the young communications rating next to Wide Boy whispered out of the side of his mouth, "it's a ruddy pierhead jump! We've bin shanghaied. If this is the *Rose,* I'm getting a draft chit out of her toot sweet!"

Wide Boy grimly nodded his agreement.

Degenhardt's smile vanished as if his jaw were worked by a steel spring. Behind him he'd heard the Captain's footsteps. His chest swelled. "Draft! *Attention!"*

The young men shuffled to a semblance of attention and stared at their new captain: a man in his late twenties or early thirties, but looking older, in spite of the jaunty angle of his salt-stained cap, young destroyer officers affected. The fading ribbons of the D.S.C. and D.S.O. on his chest showed he'd seen plenty of action these last years; yet his eyes were not hard like those of his Chief Petty Officer. He regarded them compassionately, almost sadly, but his little speech of welcome was dry and businesslike enough, ending with the words: "the repairs to the *Rose* are nearly finished. Now we can expect that their Lordships will soon ensure that we'll be returning to sea duty. Time then, is short, You'll have to settle down and find your feet quickly. We won't have weeks, we'll have days!" Lamb flashed a quick look at the *Campbelltown* and wondered momentarily exactly what did lie ahead of them. "I shall expect you all to play your part, whether you're a stoker or a seaman, a writer or a cook. We've got a job to do. Let's do it." Commander Lamb raised a gloved hand in warning. "And God help any one of you who doesn't pull his weight. He'll be off this ship and back to the depot before he knows what's hit him. All right, Chief Petty Officer, take 'em away."

"Thank you, sir!"

As Degenhardt bellowed "dismiss!" Wide Boy's eyes gleamed suddenly. Now he knew how he was going to get that draft chit back to the Depot!

The Wide Boy's first attempt to "rock the boat", as he privately termed it was made the following day when the *Rose* ran out into the Channel with the rest of the 10th Anti-Submarine Striking Force, to test her anti-submarine drill. Two miles out, Commander Lamb ordered a simulated "ping".*

Immediately, the depth charge crews began dropping a pattern of depth charges. Great white spouts of water shot high into the grey morning air, bringing with them myriads of dead and dying fish of all varieties. Most of them were too far away for the look-outs to grab with the boathooks.

But the crew of "A" Turret on look-out duty were more fortunate. Suddenly on the port bow, they saw a huge dead cod floating within grabbing distance. "Fish and taties tonight for my mess!" Scouse MacFadden chortled happily, and grabbed for it with his boathook.

But Wide Boy was quicker off the mark. Leaning dangerously over the rail, he swept the cod into an empty fire bucket and straightening up, grinned triumphantly at the outraged Scouse. "Yer mean, fish and taties for my mess, Stripey."

"Who you calling Stripey, you no-badge shit of an AB, you?" he growled. "And I saw the bastard first."

Wide Boy grinned at the Leading Seaman provocatively. "Yer, but I was quicker, wasn't I? Yer've got to get yer finger out if you want to get on in this world, mate, yer know!"

"Yer'll get me finger in yer ruddy cheeky eye, if yer not careful, *mate!*" Scouse snarled, gripping the boathook menacingly.

"D'yer want to make anything of it?"

"D'you?"

Suddenly the two of them were going at it hammer and tongs until finally Wild Boy got sick of the argument. "So you want the sodding kipper, d'yer?" he cried angrily.

"It's ruddy well mine anyhow," Scouse yelled back.

* The signal of the asdic that a submarine had been sighted.

"Okay, then take the ruddy thing!" Wide Boy bellowed and swinging the big cod with all his strength, slapped it wetly across Scouse's face, sending him flying across the desk. And as he lay there, spluttering terrible obscenities, Wide Boy draped the fish artistically across his chest and strolled casually back to his post.

That morning he gained an implacable enemy.

Two days later, back in Plymouth, Chief Petty Officer Degenhardt opened the Request Book in front of Lieutenant Doan, who was in charge of that morning's request men, and shouted as if he were taking the parade at Devonport Naval Barracks: "First Request is by Leading Seaman MacFadden, sir!"

Doan looked slightly pained. He pressed his right hand delicately to his temple and said: "Could we tone it down to a soft roar, Coxswain? I was on the pink gin last night. Please!"

"Sir!" Degenhardt bellowed and without pause commanded. "Leading Seaman MacFadden — three paces forward — *march!*" Scouse, cap tucked firmly under his right armpit, his face grim and pale, save for the green swelling at the end of his big nose, stepped forward smartly. Degenhardt glanced down at the Request Book, while Scouse stared fiercely into nothing. "Leading Seaman MacFadden requests to see the First Officer, sir, to obtain permission to have a grudge fight with Able Seaman Stevens."

Doan forgot his hangover and last night's unsuccessful encounter with a Wren officer in a Plymouth bar, who had decided after a great many gins-and-tonic that he wasn't sufficiently adorned with gold braid to deserve her undoubted sexual charms. "What's that, MacFadden?" he demanded.

Scouse caught himself just in time. "Stevens half-hooked the end of me NAAFI banger, sir," he said with restrained emotion.

Doan looked appealingly at Degenhardt. "What did he say, Chief?"

"Stevens stole the end of his NAAFI sausage," Degenhardt translated for the puzzled American First-Lieutenant.

"Oh," Doan said, slightly bewildered by the whole affair. "Is that important enough for you to want to fight this guy — er — Stevens?"

"Ay, ay, sir, it is," Scouse said determinedly. "Yer see, sir, in the leading seamen's mess we don't go much on pusser's bangers. They don't have ends like the NAAFI bangers do. So we club together to buy NAAFI bangers — out of our brass."

Doan sighed and looked at Degenhardt again. "For God's sake, translate please, Chief!"

"It's like this, sir. Issue sausages ain't got skins. The NAAFI ones have. When you puncture them, the ends come out and the cooks can get them nice and crispy. Apparently Leading Seaman MacFadden is partial to those ends —"

"Yer," Scouse interrupted the CPO angrily, "and that sod Stevens has been nicking my ends. Yesterday morning and this morning agen. I'd just turned me back to ask me oppo Bunts what was gonna win the Cheltenham, and when I turned back, my ends was gone and that bugger Stevens was grinning all over his cake-hole. And I know for why — he'd nicked me banger."

"Watch yer language in front of the officer, lad!" Degenhardt rapped.

But Scouse was beyond listening to the CPO's warning. "That's why I want to have a go at him." Scouse's face was flushed scarlet with anger, the purple vein ticking at his temple. "I demand a grudge fight, sir!"

Doan gulped. He had never been faced with a situation like this before. Of course, he could make out a charge against Stevens, but he hardly thought the Captain would take kindly to a charge sheet reading: "Did commit an act prejudicial to Good Order and Naval Discipline in that he did steal the end of one NAAFI sausage, the property of B. E. MacFadden, Leading Seaman ..." No, that wouldn't go down at all. Yet it seemed absurd to set up the facilities for a grudge fight on the upper deck in full view of the whole Anti-Sub Flotilla. It would hardly do the *Rose's* reputation much good, when it came out that two members of the ship's crew were fighting over one lousy sausage.

"All right, Leading Seaman, just step outside for a moment while I consider the matter."

"Hat on," Degenhardt barked. "Salute the officer! About turn! Quick march ... left, right, left right!" Scouse shot out of the little cabin, with Degenhardt doubling at his heels like a snapping terrier.

"Shut the door," Doan said when Degenhardt returned. "Now who is this guy Stevens? Is he one of the new draft?"

"Ay, ay, sir," Degenhardt answered. "Wide Boy, they call him among the crew. I've got my eye on him. Could be a potential lead swinger, but an excellent record from the Depot. One of the best gunners they've ever turned out from Whale Island since the start of hostilities. Or so it says on his record. And the *Rose* certainly can use good gunners."

"You can say that again, Chief," Doan agreed. He sighed and promised himself the coolest, longest beer he could find in Plymouth once the pubs were open and he was off duty. "All right, what're we gonna do about 'em?"

Degenhardt answered at once. "Let 'em get it out of their systems, sir. It's not the first time the two of them have had a run-in. Best to get it sorted out once and for all."

"Who do you think'll win, Chief?"

"Stevens's a big bloke, sir, all of six foot. But if you'll forgive my French, that MacFadden is a cunning bastard. He's been around from the Pompey Hard to the Persian Gulf. I think once MacFadden's been in the ring with him for a couple of rounds, we'll have no more trouble from Wide Boy Stevens, sir. And we do need all the good gunners we can get."

"Okay," Doan said. "Wheel him in again, Chief."

Dutifully Degenhardt "wheeled" in a red-faced MacFadden, and Doan, trying to look more serious than he felt, snapped: "All right. Request granted, MacFadden. Tomorrow, fifteen hundred hours on the upper deck."

"Thank you, sir," MacFadden said, his face lighting up, a sudden unholy look in his eyes, which Doan didn't like one bit.

"But remember this, MacFadden, I'm gonna be there personally to see all's fair, square and above board. Get it?"

"Ay, ay, sir." MacFadden's face went serious again, but the unholy light did not vanish from his eyes.

*"Hat on,"* Degenhardt commanded. *"Request granted, fifteen-hundred hours, upper deck, tomorrow, salute officer, about turn, double ..."*

Doan slumped back in his chair, as the two of them marched out, all stamping hobnail boots and wildly swinging arms, and groaned. "Who", he asked himself, "would be the First Officer on the HMS *Rose* on a morning like this?"

# THREE

But Lieutenant Doan was not fated to attend the MacFadden-Stevens grudge fight the next afternoon. Two hours after he had finished with his morning duties and was beginning to lick his dry lips in anticipation of that first, delightful, cool pint — the hair of the dog — a dust-covered dispatch rider in Army khaki screeched to a halt on the wet jetty opposite HMS *Rose*. A big, burly "Gestapoman" — a member of the naval police — who had suddenly begun to patrol the naval docks that morning for some unknown reason, checked the man's credentials and then directed him up the gangplank to the lower deck. There, Chief Petty Officer Degenhardt took charge of him, and led him directly to the Captain. Five minutes later, Doan was summoned to the Captain's cabin at the double."

"What's up, skipper?" Doan panted, opening the cabin door, "you been given command of the *Prince of Wales* or something?"

"Not exactly, Doan," Lamb answered, folding up the signal and tucking it away carefully inside his jacket. "But it's something to do with royalty all right."

"What do you mean, sir?"

"Better start practising your curtsey — we're going to meet King George's cousin."

"Eh!"

Lt Commander Lamb grinned at the puzzled First Lieutenant. "Yes, we've just been summoned to visit Lord Louis Mountbatten's HQ in Richmond Terrace this evening."

"Oh, for crying out loud — not the Commando HQ!" Doan exclaimed.

"Right in one, I'm afraid. The balloon's about to go up once more..."

They were all assembled there when Lamb and Doan arrived at the Combined Operations HQ in London; for some it could mean the Victoria Cross and others death before the month was out. The briefing-room was packed with familiar and unfamiliar faces, officers in the blue of the Royal Navy and the khaki of every commando currently stationed in the United Kingdom, plus the darker uniform of the Free French Commando.

As the two of them took their seats next to a bearded Commander Beattie, the skipper of the *Campbelltown,* Doan winked significantly and whispered to Lamb: "It looks as if the whole gang is here, skipper."

Lamb nodded in return. It certainly did. Now he knew for certain that the balloon was about to go up. Five minutes later, Commodore First Class Mountbatten's first words confirmed that he had guessed right. "Gentlemen," he announced, standing tall, erect, and handsome on the little stage in the front of the big low room, "let me say this, right from the outset. This is not an ordinary raid. It is an operation of war!"

An electric ripple of excitement went through his audience. Now the assembled officers realized why they had been called so suddenly from all over the United Kingdom for this conference. Obviously the lot of them, naval and army officers, were going to be engaged in some sort of a combined operations mission.

Mountbatten clicked his fingers. Behind him an aide drew the curtain covering the wall map. His audience craned their necks forward to try to make out the harbour which was suddenly revealed. Mountbatten let the suspense build for a moment and then with a fine sense of theatre said loudly, "Gentlemen, the port of St Nazaire, which is to be the target of the 10th Anti-Submarine Striking Force, at a date which I will reveal to you later."

Suddenly the whole room was alive with excited chatter and comment, while Mountbatten stood there in silence, hands dug deep

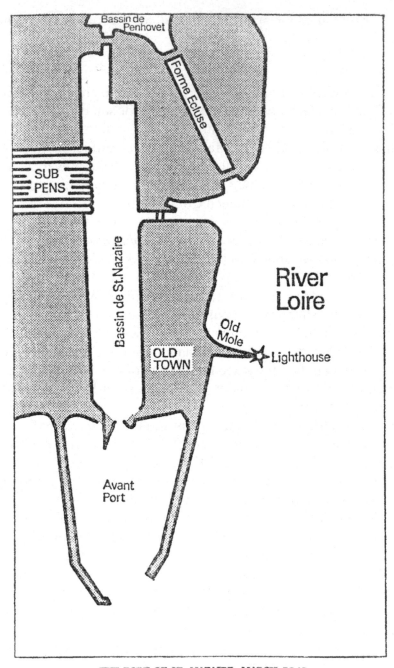

THE PORT OF ST. NAZAIRE, MARCH 1942

into his tunic pockets, watching their faces half-amused, half quizzical.

Then, without looking round, he clicked his fingers, and the same aide who had drawn back the curtain from the map, slipped a pointer dutifully into his master's elegantly manicured hand. "If I may have your attention, gentlemen," Mountbatten said with quick authority and tapped the big map with the pointer.

The chatter died away at once.

"St Nazaire, gentlemen, where the River Loire joins the Atlantic, a city of some fifty thousand souls and two hundred and fifty miles from the nearest British port, Falmouth ..." Swiftly he explained how the *Bismarck* had attempted and failed to reach the port in the previous May and how the Premier feared that her sister ship the *Tirpitz* would try to do the same, after she sailed from her Norwegian refuge.

"Now it is *our* task, gentlemen," he continued, "to make sure that the *Tirpitz* never leaves her present berth, by destroying St Nazaire's port facilities. Now how are we going to do that?" Quickly Mountbatten answered his own question. "By destroying the great dry dock, *Forme Ecluse* — here — or more accurately the big gates — here — which give access to it. Once that is done, there is no other port on the Atlantic seaboard capable of taking the *Tirpitz.*" Mountbatten allowed himself a brief smile. "And to make sure that we don't find the whole op too boring, the PM has decreed that we set ourselves as our secondary objective, the destruction of the sub pens already constructed or in process of being constructed — here — off the *Bassin de St Nazaire.* Just to ensure we don't break into a run, as it were."

Mountbatten allowed them a moment to absorb the information before he continued. "Now what are the difficulties?" he asked rhetorically.

"I could goddam well tell him —" Doan began, but his whispered comment was drowned by Mountbatten's reply to his own question. "One. The port of St Nazaire is exactly six miles up the River Loire. Let me repeat that — *six miles up the Loire.* That is six miles deeper into German-occupied territory than any Combined

Ops coastal raid ever attempted since the Commandos were formed. That is why I call this, *not* a raid, but an operation of war."

Again Mountbatten allowed the assembled officers to absorb the information, but this time the faint smile was missing from his lips.

"Now difficulty number two — the approach. The approach to the St Nazaire docks is by a deep water channel running under the lee of the north bank of the River Loire — and most of its length is defended by heavy coastal batteries. South of that channel there is a wide expanse of mud flats, covered only at high tide. According to the boffins, the high spring tide at the end of March would give us just enough water for motor launches — and destroyers, providing they weren't too heavily laden."

Doan looked significantly at Lamb. Lamb gave him a slight incline of the head; he had begun to realize too, what their potential role in the operation might be.

"Finally," Mountbatten went on, "difficulty number three. The distance the attack force would have to cover — and bear in mind the range of the average motor launch. The nearest harbour to St Nazaire would be — here — at Falmouth in Cornwall. That would mean a round trip of five hundred miles! Naturally, there is a very real possibility that the Boche might discover the attack force on the way out and, of course, they would be in an excellent position to harass the force when it starts back."

"*If* it starts back", Doan thought, but he kept that particular thought strictly to himself. He had served in the Royal Navy long enough to know that even the most irreverent of its members preferred to exercise the stiff upper lip at such moments.

Mountbatten cleared his throat. "Well, gentlemen, those are the difficulties. Let us see what we propose to do about them, shall we?" He extended his hand towards a burly, moustached Commando colonel sitting in the front row of the audience. "Colonel Newman would you like to take over, now?"

The Commando Colonel put out his pipe hastily and sprang on to the stage with surprising agility for a man of his age and bulk; he was obviously very fit.

"Thank you, sir," he nodded to Mountbatten and then faced his audience. Well, gentlemen, let me say this from the outset. The chap who planned this op deserves the DSO for his damned audacity." He grinned at the assembled officers and they grinned back. Colonel Newman was obviously a character.

"All right. Now what's the drill as far as the Army goes? This is the answer. Men from my own Second Commando and another eighty from every commando in the UK, each man a demolitions expert, will sail to St Nazaire with the aid of the Royal." He grinned down at Lt Commander Ryder, the Commander of the 10th Anti-Submarine Striking Force, obviously pleased at being able to put the Royal Navy firmly in its place as mere means of transport for conveying the real fighting men to the scene of the action. "There, while the RAF bombs the port to create a diversion, they will land from the launches. It will be their task to put out the coastal batteries, destroy the sub pens, and generally raise bloody hell in the dock area. That will be the role of the Commando." Without further words he dropped off the platform, took his seat and lit his pipe again, as if he had never moved from his hard wooden government issue chair.

Mountbatten stood up and said: "Thank you, Colonel Newman. Now Commander Ryder, can I call on you to explain the Navy's part in this operation?"

Ryder, a good-looking officer with an aggressive jaw, took his time to mount the rostrum. Once there, he dug his hands deep in his pockets and stared around in silence for a moment, as if he were surveying a particularly sloppy ship's crew from his own quarterdeck. Then he cleared his throat noisily, as if signalling to them to pay attention and began. "The Navy's role. One, HMS *Campbelltown,* commanded by Commander Beattie, will ram the dock gate at the *Forme Ecluse."* Ryder ignored the excited buzz of chatter which greeted his remark, and he continued without pause. "Of course," he said drily, "ramming dock gates is not the sort of thing that one can practise very frequently, so we cannot be certain that the *Campbelltown* will pull it off completely. To make doubly certain, however, she will be carrying a five-ton charge of delayed high explosive. That, the boffins think, should do the job."

He cleared his throat once more. "Two. The attack force will sail in three columns. The midships column will consist of my own ship the *Atherstone,* HMS *Tynedale,* and of course, HMS *Campbelltown,* plus Motor Gun Boat 354. It will be the job of the midships column to provide any necessary fire power. The two port and starboard columns will carry Colonel Newman's commandos, two hundred and sixty-five men in all. Any questions so far?"

Lamb leaned forward attentively, with one overwhelming question in his mind. Where did HMS *Rose* fit into this business?

A moment later, Commander Ryder striding purposefully over to the map answered the question for him. "Now the naval force is faced by two major dangers, presupposing that it can get into the mouth of the Loire without being spotted. One, the coastal guns running along here from the Old Mole up to the entrance of the *Forme Ecluse.* As you've already heard, Colonel Newman's commandos will take care of those. Now danger number two. Intelligence reported yesterday that the Jerries have suddenly berthed four *Möwe* class torpedo boats — here — in the *Avant Port.* I should imagine that the TBs will present no danger to us getting *into* the Loire Estuary. But," he paused significantly, "they could provide us with plenty of trouble on the way out, if they aren't dealt with beforehand. This is where HMS *Rose* comes in. She will stand off until the main attack force is well in position —"

Doan flashed Lamb a quick look. It was obvious that the poor old *Rose* was going to be the low man on the totem pole once again. In spite of her record over the past two years, the *Rose* was still on somebody's shit-list up in the Admirality.

"Then," Ryder was saying, "she'll land thirty commandos whose job it will be to deal with the Jerry TBs. If they fail to blow them up, then and *only then,* will the *Rose* take them under fire and destroy them. As you can see, the Old Town of St Nazaire is located on the *Avant Port* and we must not cause French civilian casualties by indiscriminate gunfire."

Lamb sighed heavily and looked downcast. The *Rose* was being relegated not even to a secondary role, but to that of a damned troop transport. Would their Lordships never forget that his father, the Old Admiral, had once been court-martialed and dismissed from

40

the Navy for alleged cowardice under fire in the First War? Weren't the D.S.C. and D.S.O. he bore on his chest proof that whatever they thought of Admiral Lamb, his son had inherited none of that alleged cowardice?*

But already Commander Ryder was vacating the stage for Mountbatten. The Head of Combined Operations now summed up the operation in that swift, expert way of his, which one day would take him to the highest command in the Navy. "In essence, gentlemen, the whole operation depends on the attack force getting into position before the Boche has wakened up to the fact. Once the *Campbelltown* has rammed the dock gate and the commandos are ashore, there is little the Boche can do save *react,* for we will already have *acted.* So what does it all boil down to, gentlemen?" He paused and flashed a look around the tense room: "This: Absolute, complete security. Now the assembly harbour should be fairly safe from enemy aerial reconnaissance. Falmouth has never been visited by enemy aircraft. The danger then will not come from *above,* but from *within.* From our own men! Intelligence has therefore provided a cover story for the operation. The legend for the 10th Anti-Submarine Striking Force is that it is intended to carry out long-range anti-sub sweeps far beyond the Western Approaches. As for the Commando, as soon as they arrive at the depot ship, *Princess Josephine Charlotte* at Falmouth, tropical gear, sun helmets and so forth, will be *smuggled* aboard her at night so that the men and anyone watching her will presume the Commando is heading for the Med."

Mountbatten paused dramatically: "From this moment onwards, no soldier or sailor will be allowed to leave his unit or ship, whatever the circumstances. If there is a fatality in the man's family and the family appeals for compassionate leave for him, the appeal will be conveniently forgotten until the man returns from the operation. If anyone gets sick, he will be taken care of by his own MO or sick-berth attendant. If we suffer any fatalities during the working-up exercises in Devonport, the body will not be returned to the individual's family. It will be retained in Devonport Naval Hospital until it can be safely released for burial: I know these measures will cause hardship, perhaps some heartache. There is no

* See *Flotilla Attack* for further details.

other way." There was sudden iron in the Commodore's voice. "At this grave stage of the war, Operation Chariot is vital. *We must not fail now!*"

Mountbatten allowed them a moment to absorb the full implication of his words; then said, "Gentlemen, that is all. Good-day!"

Five minutes later they were all trooping outside into the grey London morning, aware that once again, a date with destiny had been planned for them ...

# FOUR

"Sir!" Chief Petty Officer Degenhardt barked, the Request Book tucked under his arm.

"Yes, Chief?" Doan asked, his mind elsewhere.

"First request of the morning, sir. Able Seaman Stevens." Suddenly Doan remembered the grudge fight of the previous afternoon and asked, "How did it go, Chief?"

Degenhardt's wizened monkey face cracked into a bleak smile. "Bloody — for Able Seaman Stevens. I've never seen a dirtier clean fight since I joined the Royal."

Doan grinned back. "Who refereed it then? One of the subs?"

"No, sir." Degenhardc's grin broadened. "*I did,* sir."

Doan nodded his head significantly. It figured. Indirectly Degenhardt was disciplining Stevens through Scouse MacFadden.

"All right, Chief, then wheel him in gently."

"Ay, ay, sir."

"Oh brother," Doan suppressed his gasp of surprise just in time as Degenhardt "wheeled" in Wide Boy Stevens. The young seaman's face was one livid mess. His right eye was purple and almost closed and there was a thick piece of sticking plaster running down the side of his left temple.

"What in hell's name hit you — a steam-roller?" Doan asked. "Stevens, you really took some punishment!"

Wide Boy did not answer, but the side-look he gave grinning Chief Petty Officer Degenhardt spoke volumes.

"All right, Stevens, what's the problem?"

"I want to volunteer for a battle wagon, sir," Stevens croaked nasally through nostrils still filled with dried blood. "I don't feel happy on this ship."

"And brother, you certainly don't look it," Doan told himself, but to the young seaman, he said: "And what makes you feel that, Stevens?"

"That fight yesterday, sir. I'm not mentioning no names. But me and my oppo thinks it was a put-up job. If that MacFadden didn't have a horseshoe inside his right glove, I'm a Dutchman."

"I examined the gloves personally before the contest, sir," Degenhardt snapped, staring with sphinx-like gaze at a point on the bulkhead behind Doan's left shoulder, lying without the slightest hesitation. "Everything square and above board, sir!"

"But, the bugger —"

"Watch yer tongue in front of the officer!" Degenhardt rapped.

"So you want out, Stevens." Doan said slowly. "That's a pity. You've brought an excellent record with you from Whale Island and we can sure use good gunners on board the old *Rose.*"

"Maybe, sir. But I'd still like my request to be acted on."

Doan faked a smile. "I'd like to help you, Stevens." He shrugged easily. "But unfortunately I can't. Nobody is leaving the *Rose* for the time being."

"But Regs say you've got to forward me request, sir." Stevens persisted, now looking puzzled.

"I know. It'll be forwarded all right. To the Captain. And you know what he'll do with it?"

No sir."

"He'll lose it, that's what he'll do."

At Stevens' side, Degenhardt could hardly restrain his grin. "Now then, Stevens what do you want me to do, eh?"

"You can go and f —" Stevens caught himself just in time — "forward me application for transfer to the Captain. I'll take me chance that he'll tear it up."

"As you wish, Stevens." Doan looked across at a grinning Chief Petty Officer Degenhardt. "Make a note of that in the Request Book, CPO."

"Ay, ay, sir!" Degenhardt barked. *All right, Stevens, cap on, salute-officer, about turn, double march — at the double, laddie, open yer legs, nothing'll fall out, left, right, left right left ..."*

For better or worse. Scouse MacFadden's "A" turret had retained the services of the best gunner Whale Island had turned out since 1939. HMS *Rose* was a little further on her way to being a happier ship, though, in Lt-Commander Lamb's opinion, she was a long way off being an efficient one — and time was running out fast.


As the first week of March 1942 gave way to the second, Lamb began training the draft in earnest. That week became one long, hectic, never-ending round of speed trials, practice shoots, depth charge drills, anti-aircraft shoots — and every day, slipped in so that the crew paid no particular attention to the drill — boat-loading and handling drill. Every hour of every new day seemed to bring new headaches and even more backbreaking work under the terrible conditions of the Channel in late winter; half the new draft were a permanent green colour, continually running to the side to vomit whatever they had managed to keep down of the last meal.

The first practice shoot with the new Oerlikon anti-aircraft guns, wrecked the galley; produced a great grey rat in the middle of the for'ard messdeck, who went crazy with the noise, chasing his long tail at a tremendous speed until somebody clonked him on the head with a seaboot; and baptized the ship's cat "Baa-Lamb", with a tin of golden syrup that fell from somebody's shelf.

That same day the afternoon's boat-lowering drill ended with a long boat dangling at a crazy angle from a stanchion and half the frightened crew splashing for their lives in the cold waters of the harbour to the ribald comments from the ships of the rest of the 10th Flotilla.

Even those older hands who still had the strength of an evening, after a strenuous day's back-breaking sea duty, to go ashore for a pint at one of the naval port's many pubs, could never be sure of being long enough on land to finish it. For that first week, Lamb did not hesitate to pull more than one surprise recall on his weary crew and have them doubling back to the *Rose,* steam up already,

ready to cast off wires and fenders at any moment. As a disgruntled Scouse commented to his oppo Bunts: "Ain't the Old Man gonna give us all-night-in ever agen? Yer ain't in the pub trying to chat up some Judy, for more than half a sodding dog-watch and the sodding Gestapo is rousting yer out agen, shouting their pudden heads off that the crew of HMS *Rose* has got a recall. It ain't sodding normal, I tell yer that, Bunts. The Old Man must have gone off his nut!"

But Commander Lamb, ignored the curious looks the crew shot him during his tours of the ship when they thought he wasn't looking, and the weary ditty that carried down to his cabin when the ship was finally back in Plymouth of an evening,

"Roll on the *Rodney, Nelson* and *Renown,*
This one-funnelled bastard ain't gonna get me down!"

And he knew well that the "one-funnelled bastard" their plaintive voices were referring to — was HMS *Rose.* As he confided in an unshaven,red-eyed Doan at the end of the second week as they nursed pink gins in hands blue from a long freezing day in the Channel: "I don't care if I freeze the bollocks off them, Doan. I've got to knock them into shape before Mountbatten blows the whistle on us. We can't afford any slip-ups on the day from inefficiency. I'm not prepared to take any more guff from the others about the *Rose* being jinxed."

Doan nodded morosely and sipped his pink gin without comment. He knew that Lamb had almost a love affair with the *Rose,* his first command after fourteen years' service in the Royal Navy. An insult to the ageing slow destroyer, the only one of her class and far slower than the two Hunt class destroyers which made up the rest of the 10th Flotilla, was like calling his genteel, widowed mother, the pillar of Eastbourne's middle-class society, a whore.

Rapidly the new men started to settle in, helped by the old hands, who knew now from the "buzzes" circulating throughout dockyard pubs, that it wouldn't be long before the *Rose* saw action again. On Wednesday of the third week when four successive crews of draftees had taken more than five minutes to lower a whaler and row around a buoy a hundred yards from the ship, an angry Lamb called for a volunteer crew of old hands to man the whaler, and got more than he could accommodate. With himself as a stroke oar, the "stripeys", many of them three-badge able seamen in their early forties, not the usual type of sailor to volunteer for anything, lowered the whaler and rowed round the buoy and back in just over two minutes. They were received back at the *Rose,* crimson-faced and gasping like elderly asthmatics, to be greeted by three cheers from the rest of the admiring crew.

That same week, Lamb started to hear the first good reports of the draftees from his petty officers. "Ay, Captain," the Scots ER.9, in charge of the engine-room, confided in his thick Glaswegian accent, wiping his oil-stained hands on cotton waste, "yon new laddies is no so canny as the old mob, but they're a wee bit better than I thought." That coming from ER.9 Graham, with thirty years' service behind him, was high praise indeed.

Scouse MacFadden did not lag behind when Lamb checked with him in "A" Turret that same afternoon. "Well, sir, they're not exactly Robin Hoods, 'ceps that big lad from the Smoke, Stevens, but they're shaping up right well. They've even learned not to shoot on a forward roll now. And that ain't bad for a bunch of sprogs, sir, who ain't never been to sea before, is it, sir?"

And Lt Commander Lamb had to agree that it wasn't too bad for "a bunch of sprogs".


By now the *Rose* herself was wild with "buzzes". "We're going up north to Scapa," they said, "so you'd better get ready, you sprogs, to start liking sheep — and I don't mean cooked on the table!"

"It's the Med, lads," they said, "I got it from a bloke in the 'Mucky Duck' — the 'Black Swan' to you HO sprogs — who's got a brother in the Pusser's Department. They're issuing tropical gear. We're all off to get our knees brown."

And they said, "Ner, yer all talking a load of old bull. We're off on the convoys agen. Watching out that them fat Yankee generals in Grosvenor Square, can fill their guts with ice cream and fried chicken!"

But when on Friday, March 20th, thirty burly heavily-laden commandos, descended from Bedford three-tonners on the quay below, and began to plod up the gangplank behind a slim, young moustached Lieutenant, with — of all things — a broadsword stuck in his webbing belt, they knew that all the "buzzes" were completely incorrect. They were sailing neither west, north nor south. With a sinking feeling they realized that the commandos signified one thing only — they would soon be sailing across that short stretch of grey-green, heaving water which separated them from German Occupied Europe!

As Scouse, his normal good humour gone, remarked darkly to his favourite oppo, Bunts, the *Rose's* leading signaller: "It looks, old lad, as if the *Rose* is off to the wars agen." He sniffed. "And right sodding soon!"

But Scouse MacFadden was not quite right for a change. The overage destroyer was not going to the wars — just yet. There was still one little preliminary to be taken care of first before that happened.

# FIVE

"This is the captain!" Commander Lamb's voice echoed metallically over the loudspeakers, drowning the roar and crash of the mountainous waves and even the banshee-howl of the gale-force wind, "I shall now tell you the purpose of this exercise." Down below, another of the green-faced, hollow-eyed commandos, who were going to play the most important part in the forthcoming exercise, could wait to hear no more. With his fist stuffed in his mouth and making strange chocking noises deep in his throat, he ran crazily for the heads already filled with others of his sea-sick comrades.

"We have been asked — that is the 10th Anti-Strike Force — to help to test Devonport's anti-invasion defences by the Army Command. Each ship in the Tenth will have a separate task. Ours will be to land the commandos inside the Sound, opposite the Light Ship. It won't be easy in this kind of weather, but I expect every man to do the best he can — and remember all coastal forces, plus the fishing fleet and the Home Guard, have been alerted and are on the look-out for us. That is all." There was a sudden metallic click and the tannoys went dead.

Scouse nudged Wide Boy, who was leaning against the gleaming brass breech of the 5-inch gun in "A" turret looking very pale and a little wild-eyed. "Exercise! Did you hear that, Wide Boy? The Skipper should pull the other one. It's got bells on it!"

"What do you mean, Scouse?" Wide Boy asked and gulped hastily, as the green bile rose in his throat once again. For a moment the *Rose* seemed to be floating in mid-air.

"I mean," Scouse said, as the *Rose* came down again with a crash that made the 5-incher's breech tremble wildly at Wide Boy's back, "this bugger's a dress-rehearsal for what we're gonna do on yon side. We're gonna land the commandos. And there'll be a ruddy lot of hairy-arsed Jerries waiting for us there, wherever it is. Yer can bet yer bottom dollar on it."

"Fer ferk's sake, gimme the bucket," Wide Boy gasped wildly, feeling the hot vomit filling his throat. At that particular moment, he didn't give a bugger whether the whole of the Jerry Army was waiting for them on the other side. All he wanted was for the *Rose* to stop going up and down, as if it were on a ruddy switchback. Smiling understandingly, Scouse handed him the pail with a flourish, as if he were giving him the crown jewels.


But the gale continued all the way to Devonport, and the commandos, in spite of their training, turned out to be very bad sailors. They lay on the upper deck, supposedly ready to plunge ashore with elan and energy, in dumb, green-faced misery. Their young commander, Lieutenant Wall-Jones, tried to put a brave face on it, fighting valiantly against his own seasickness. But after a huge dark wave had nearly sucked him off the deck on his way to the bridge, he succumbed to the urgent signals from his stomach and heaved his guts up.

Up on the streaming bridge, hanging on grimly to the chart-table, Lamb shook his head and said to a grinning Doan, "You know I think Operation Vivid is going to turn out one hell of a balls-up. And take that bloody grin off your face, Doan, can't you!"

"Ay, ay, sir. Anything you say, sir. But brother, those brown jobs really are a sight for sore eyes. It's many a year since I've seen so much concentrated misery in such a small area."

"Wait till you see the look on our own faces at tomorrow morning's post-mortem, Doan," Lamb said severely and turned his attention to manoeuvring the heaving, bucking *Rose* through the howling gale, into the Sound and on to their objective.

Commander Lamb's gloomy prognosis turned out to be all too accurate. Almost from the very start, unknown to the *Rose's* captain, the vital exercise became a complete failure.

Navigation on the motor-launches carrying the main wave of the Second Commando, was terrible. Two of them ran aground on the mud-flats just off the harbour, and by the time they got clear in the tearing gale with visibility down to twenty feet, their captains had lost their sense of direction completely.

Another group was separated from the midships' column of destroyers and missed the entrance to the estuary altogether, finishing up forlornly, miles outside the exercise area.

Commander Ryder's destroyer column, minus the *Campbelltown,* managed to fight the gale and penetrate the Sound, before their luck ran out. Just off Oreston, the other Hunt class destroyer, HMS *Tynedale,* almost collided with one of the local fishing boats. Its skipper, already warned about the exercise and like all fishermen always eager to take a rise out of the Royal, signalled the shore immediately that he had sighted the "enemy". Minutes later the coastal batteries on both sides of the Sound were bringing their guns to bear on the destroyers steaming through the gale, and the umpires judged that the destroyer force had been "wiped out".

HMS *Rose* proved luckier than the rest of the 10th Flotilla. She found the spot where she was to land the commandos without being detected, and after some difficulties, managed to launch the whalers, filled with groaning, vomiting commandos. With pleasure, Lamb watched how his draftees and old hands fought the off-shore swell, putting their whole energy behind it, fighting the waves every yard of the way. "By God, Doan," he said enthusiastically to the American First Lieutenant, "they're really shaping up at last!"

"Famous last words, sir!" Doan replied, as Chief Petty Officer Degenhardt's lead whaler hit the shore and the first commandos springing overboard went skidding across the slick mudflat as if they were on an ice-rink. Willya get a load o' that!"

"Oh, hell!" Lamb groaned, as Lieutenant Wall-Jones, sword raised high above his head, lost his balance on the mud. His feet went from under him. His sword flew into the air and next moment he sprawled full length in the stinking goo, as helpless as a baby. As Petty Officer Degenhardt bent down to give him a hand, his feet went from under him, too. Like a comedian in an old slap-stick silent movie, he did a pratfall and sat down suddenly on his skinny rump, a look of absolute disgust on his monkey's face.

"Don't let me look!" Lamb cried, as man after man lost his grip on the slick mud, shouting with rage as they tried to get to their feet again, failing lamentably. "My God, what an absolute, ruddy balls-up!"

Time and time again, the commandos, lathered with thick clinging black mud from head to toe, tried to scale the sheer slick wall of the mud flat, slipping down helplessly as they lost their grip yet again. The morning air was thick with their angry curses.

Finally, Lieutenant Wall-Jones, minus his stocking-cap and sword, managed to get to the top on the backs of a pyramid of his gasping, mud-grimed men to be confronted by an elderly, Home Guard, with the ribbons of the Boer War on his chest.

The old man gave him a toothless grin and levelled his rifle at crestfallen Wall-Jones' head. "We was supposed to be on the lookout for Jerries," he croaked asthmatically. "But you lot look more like a bunch of black minstrels!"

He laughed hysterically at his own humour.

On the *Rose's* bridge, watching the episode through his binoculars, Lamb groaned and said: "Mountbatten'll hit the ceiling when he hears about this one!"

# SIX

*"Miss Mary Bridget O'Sullivan, Normandy Avenue, Barnet, was fined a total of ten pounds, plus two guineas' costs far permitting bread to be wasted. It was stated that her servant was twice seen throwing bread to birds in the garden. When interviewed, she admitted that bread was put out every day. "I cannot see the poor birds starve" she said.*

"Turn that damned thing off!" Lord Louis Mountbatten's clipped voice cut incisively into the news item.

As the assembled officers shuffled to their feet to welcome the Commodore, a rating turned off the conference room's radio. The Home News died abruptly.

Mountbatten acknowledged their salute curtly. "All right, sit down, please!" he snapped, his usual pleasant smile and the "gentlemen" with which he usually greeted them, absent this cold, blustery March morning.

Doan nudged a stony-faced Lamb and whispered. "Now's when the shit hits the fan, skipper."

Lamb did not reply. He was bracing himself for the homily which undoubtedly he and HMS *Rose* would soon receive from the pale-faced, angry Prince.

But fortunately, Mountbatten's invective was reserved for the other captains and the commando officers. Swiftly and incisively, the Head of Combined Operations, detailed their failings and oversights. The young subs who skippered the MLs had shown that they hadn't "learnt a thing about navigation at King Alfred".* The commandos weren't sufficiently sea-trained — they had been "little better than a bunch of broken-down land lubbers". As for the destroyer captains, they had not shown sufficient presence of mind when challenged by the fishing-boat skipper; they should have attempted to bluff their way by him some way or other.

Mountbatten paused for what seemed a long time, while the commando and naval officers looked at the floor shame-faced. When he spoke again, his face was once more warmed by the famous Mountbatten smile. "All right, so the lot of you made a balls-up. Splendid!"

They all looked up in astonishment.

"Yes, you heard correctly. I said — *splendid.* You will undoubtedly have learned a great deal from your mistakes and won't make them again on the actual operation." He lowered his voice. "If you do, you won't survive to have to undergo another rollocking from me, will you?"

They smiled at that.

"So let's forget Operation Vivid. It's old history. Let us turn our attention to Operation Chariot, the real thing. Firstly, the whole force will move to Falmouth, at first light tomorrow." He smiled at Colonel Newman. "But let me say that your chaps will *not* be going by sea. They'll take the land route."

"Thank God for that, sir," Colonel Newman said, taking the dig in good heart, as well as the laughter of the naval officers all around him. "I think my lads have had their bellyful of life on the ocean waves, for the time being!"

Mountbatten smiled for an instant, then he was deadly serious. "Gentlemen, the Prime Minister has now set a date for Operation Chariot. You will sail from Falmouth on the afternoon of Thursday March 26th. The attack itself will start on the morning of Saturday at approximately zero one thirty hours. Now all that remains for me to do — is to wish you good luck and happy landings ..."

* Officers' training school.

"And we'll need it, sir," Doan said, as they stood outside the HQ, watching the blue-painted naval staff cars edging forward to pick up the waiting officers and transport them to the South-Western railway station and the train which would bear them back to Plymouth.

"Need what?" Lamb snapped absently, his mind full of the details of the Operation.

Doan did not answer until the pretty Wren driver in the car behind them had closed the door, effectively preventing any eavesdropping on her part. "Good luck, sir ... Good luck for the new op!"

Lamb took his gaze off a line of drab women, queuing with their shopping baskets outside a dingy butchers' shop with its notice *"Kidney or Liver Today — Ration Books A to H"*. He turned to Doan. "Is it that bad?" he asked.

"Worse," Doan answered in his direct, no-nonsense American manner "Look how it figures. One," unconsciously Doan adopted Mountbatten's manner of briefing his subordinates, "those snotties in charge of the launches will make a cock-up of their navigation, if they're ever separated from the destroyer column. We saw that yesterday."

Lamb nodded silently.

"Two. While we were sitting there, I worked out the timing his Lordship gave us. About thirty-odd hours. As Falmouth's some 250 miles from St Nazaire, that'll give us an average speed of fourteen knots, slower than some old tub of a coaster, and easy meat for a Jerry sub or E-boat. Three, even if we do make it — on target and without discovery — what about the brown jobs?"

"What *about* the brown jobs, er, the commandos?"

"Well, you saw how the poor bastards spilled their cookies yesterday as soon as we hit rough weather. Who can guarantee we won't run into the same kind of weather on the day?" He shrugged. "And what price the rough, tough, brown jobs then? Hell, if they ran into anything like that mud bank yesterday in the shape they were in, it would be curtains for them."

"All right, all right, Doan," Lamb snapped, irritated by the way the young American was putting into words all his own fears about the operation, since the abysmal failure of Operation Vivid. "What can we do about it, you bleeding ray of sunshine? Do you expect me to inform Lord Louis that his great plan stinks?"

"No, sir. There is no stopping the wheels once they're in action. I learned that before the war — *your* war — when I was an aide to that fancy-pants Admiral in Washington in '39. But we *can* make provisions for the *Rose* at least, so that *we* don't make a complete balls-up of the Op, skipper."

"What provisions had you in mind?"

The staff car stopped at a red light. Over the pretty Wren's shoulder Lamb caught a glimpse of the painted scrawl on the fruiterer's window. It read:

"Wreaths and Crosses — No Tomatoes"

He shuddered, as if the words were to be an omen of what was to come on the 27th, and then settled back to listen to Doan's eager explanation of what he meant by "provisions".


Lieutenant Doan was not the only one making "provisions" that particular March midday. Nearly a hundred and fifty miles away in Plymouth, Wide Boy Stevens had tramped the length of the bomb-shattered city centre, down George Street, through Princess Square, and Bedford Street, looking in at each surviving pub before moving on again when he realized the men he was looking for weren't present. Finally, when he was about to give up, telling himself that the crew of the new American destroyer which had docked in Plymouth that dawn had not yet got shore-leave, he spotted some of them in a dirty little pub at the bottom half of Union Street: three of them in the hip-length overcoats they wore, with the legend "USS *Grant*" prominent on the black caps worn on the backs of their crewcut heads. "Yanks," he told himself, pushing open the swing door. "In the Royal, they'd be straight inside for giving away the name of their ship like that."

Confidently, knowing that this time he was going to pull it off, he strode over to them. He planted himself next to them at the beer-stained bar and snapped at the brassy barmaid, with hennaed pompadour and red-and-white powder war-mask, "pull us a half o' best bitter, luv. I'm so dry, I could sup up the English Channel."

The barmaid pretended to be too busy with the whisky she was pouring for the biggest American sailor, who was carelessly holding a five pound note in his fingers, as if he might light his cigar with it if someone didn't relieve him of it soon.

"Got cloth-ears, ducks?" Wide Boy said carelessly, calculating that he'd slug the big one first and then let the two smaller Yanks start the action; they looked tough enough to keep going until the Gestapo rolled up and halled him to the jail at Guz. "Or don't you speak English in this place?"

The barmaid continued to fill the glass, then slid it across the counter towards the big American. "There you are, sir. Your double."

The American thrust the five pound note at her. "Buy yourself a drink, sister," he said expansively. "Or ain't this funny money enough?"

"Of course, sir." The barmaid rang up the price and added ten shillings for her own drink, three times the normal price for a double whisky.

Wide Boy repeated his order and again she ignored him, as she leaned forward to give the three American sailors a grandstand view of her admirable cleavage. "You be doing a bit of sight-seeing in Plymouth, gents?" she asked, and simpered.

"We've just started, sister," the big sailor said and guffawed. "And the view sure ain't bad from here."

The other two, although their open jackets revealed jumpers heavy with medal ribbons, didn't look much older than Wide Boy himself, and laughed a little uneasily.

The barmaid giggled. "You Yanks ain't half awful," she said and lowered her gaze with the modesty of a virgin she had not been these thirty years.

"Cor ferk a duck!" Wide Boy exploded. "Has a bloke got to stand here all bloody day waiting for a jar and being insulted in his own country, while a lot of sodding refugees from Pearl Harbour soak up all the ruddy beer?"

The barmaid appeared to become aware of his presence for the first time. "Now you watch your language, matelot," she snapped in the accent of her native Devon, "or I'll have the landlord on yer."

"Ya want some suds, sailor?" the big American asked easily and pushed another five pound note across the wet counter at the barmaid. "Have one on me."

"Who asked you to chime in, mate?" Wide Boy said aggressively, already noting the spot in the American's fat, blue-clad belly he would hit when the fun started. "In England, we don't accept drinks from strangers!"

"Sure, sure," the American said. "I read it in the book they handed out back on the ship about you limeys. What did it say, guys?"

"If Britons sit on trains without striking up conversation with you," the smallest of the three Americans said, obviously quoting from memory, "it doesn't mean they are being haughty or unfriendly. Probably they are paying more attention to you then you think."

"Bollocks!" Wide Boy said unfeelingly.

The big American's grin vanished slowly. "I suppose you know, sailor, them's fighting words?" He is levered his bulk up from the bar stool. The barmaid, well experienced in the ways of sailors fled to the back of the bar.

The Wide Boy's head was already full of the scene to come when the Guz Gestapo, summoned by the barmaid's frantic telephone call, would come bursting into the pub, to carry him off to the nick where he could relax and wait for his court-martial, while the *Rose* sailed away to carry out her mission on the other side of the Channel. In the meantime he placed his back to the bar and measured out the distance between his right fist and the Yank's fat belly. "Did you say something, fat arse?" he asked easily.

"Who you calling fat-ass?" the American said hotly, reaching forward for the empty bottle of whisky and hefting it in his big hand, neck downwards.

"You, *fat arse!*"

The American lunged forward. Too late. Wide Boy hit him in the guts. His fist seemed to travel a long way before it stopped at something hard. The American groaned low, expelling the air between his gritted teeth like a punctured tyre. Slowly his knees began to give beneath him. Wide Boy hastened the process. Clubbing both his hands he brought them down at the back of the American's bent head. He went to the floor with a loud thud, as if he had been pole-axed.

"Hey," the smaller of the American seamen said, "buddy, that ain't goddam fair —"

His words ended in a yell of pain as Wide Boy hit him across the face, crying as he did so, "Well, try that one on for size, mate!"

In an instant, all hell was let loose. The other American, who had up to now not said a word, hurtled a bottle at the big mirror behind the bar, smashing it to smithereens and setting the barmaid off screaming hysterically. He dived for Wide Boy.

The British sailor managed to avoid the knee aimed at his groin in time. But he couldn't dodge the follow-up punch directed at his chin. His head snapped back and he staggered against the bar, red and green stars exploding in front of his eyes. The two Americans yelled with triumph. The smaller one swung behind Wide Boy who desperately tried to heel him between the legs. The American dodged smartly, grabbed Wide Boy's arms and pinioned them behind his back. "I've got him, Rocky!" he cried exuberantly. "Slug him!"

Rocky needed no urging. His big right fist sank into Wide Boy's exposed defenceless stomach, brutally. Wide Boy gasped with agony. "You bastard," he cried. "Wait till I get —"

His words died suddenly in a yelp of pain, as the one called Rocky slugged him hard in the face. He felt something burst in his nose, and his chin was flooded with hot blood. Yet in spite of the acute pain, he was filled with a sudden feeling of triumph as from far, far away he began to hear the shrill gong of a police car, coming to sort the mess out. It was the Gestapo! The barmaid had called them, just as he had planned she would. As Rocky hit him again and the red and white blinding lights flashed back and forth in front of his darkening eyes, Wide Boy Stevens felt suddenly happy. He had pulled it off. HMS-bloody-*Rose* would sail without him, and in due course, when he had served his fifty-six days in the naval glass house, he would join the battlewagon where the pickings were. He'd end the war a rich man yet.

But his luck was out. Just as Rocky hit him for the third time and sent his head swinging from side to side, as if it were on springs, a familiar voice called from the door, "Get yer bleeding Yankee mitts off'n me mucker, or I'll have yer sodding guts fer garters!"

"Ferkit!" Wide Boy groaned, as he started to slide down the side of the bar, now that he was unsupported. It was Scouse!

Slumped on the floor, Wide Boy heard the sounds of battle — shattered glass, curses, frantic groans, the thump-thump of a hard fist hitting softer flesh — from far, far away, as if it were all happening in another world. Then there was the heavy thud of a body shooting to the saw-dust covered floor. Next to him, an American voice said wearily, "Oh, great balls of fire —" ending abruptly, as a heavy naval boot stomped on the side of his face. A moment later there was the sound of many glasses splintering, followed by a wild scream, then utter silence, broken only by the ever-louder sound of the police gong somewhere outside.

"Gimme yer flipper, Wide Boy," Scouse gasped. "Smartish! The sodding Gestapo's only a street away."

Wide Boy opened his eyes. Through a reddish haze, he could see Scouse's smiling, sweat-lathered face staring down at him encouragingly. "Ferk off," he said wearily. "Just let me lay here, Scouse!"

"Bugger that fer a lark, Wide Boy. This place is like a knocking house in the Snake Pit on pay-night! They'll have yer in the nick for life for this. Come on, mate!" He bent down, gasping with the effort of the slugging match, and lifted a groggy Stevens to his feet. "Come on, we'll get out through the lays."

Exactly one minute later the Gestapo and the middle-aged Plymouth civilian policemen came charging through the pub's swing doors into the glass-littered battlefield of what had once been a pub, where lay three very unconscious American seamen. By then Scouse was lugging a very reluctant Wide Boy through the tight lavatory window into the dirty cobbled alley behind the public house. Wide

Boy Stevens' last attempt to get off HMS *Rose* had failed lamentably. Now he would have to accept his fate with the rest ...

# SEVEN

Carefully Lt-Commander Lamb changed into a clean undershirt and shorts, knowing that he stood less chance of a gangrene infection if he were hit and the cotton cloth forced into the wound by the impact, was clean. Elsewhere on the *Rose,* its engines already throbbing and impatient to be underway, grey-haired, experienced Stripeys would be doing the same, tucking steel shaving mirrors in the breast pockets of their overalls for good measures and perhaps padding out their crotch — just in case!

Outside, the young Commando officer Wall-Jones was giving his men a last lecture on tactics. "Keep the moon behind you — you can control your own shadow like that and merge it with the others. Watch out for fruit trees. They usually harbour lots of birds, who'll set up a hell of a racket if they're disturbed ... Steady shuffling through the grass won't disturb them, but the slightest tinkle of metal will cause a flurry ..."

A little further on, Scouse, helped by his new mate, Stevens, whose bruised face still showed that he had been in the wars again recently, were stripping the 5-incher's firing mechanism for one last time, while the Liverpudlian Leading Seaman was singing the monotonously idiotic song of that spring:

> "She's the girl that makes the thing that
> drills the hole that holds the spring ... That
> drives the rod that turns the knob that
> works the thingumebob — that's going to
> win the war ..."

62

Lamb, slipping into his navy-blue battle-blouse, thought the damned tune would never end. Fastening his buttons, he closed his mind to the song and went out on to the deck.

The main force of ships was already beginning to crawl down the channel towards the open sea. Formed up in three columns, with the motor launches on the outside and the destroyer force led by the camouflaged *Campbelltown* in the middle, they were already picking up speed, while the Spitfires roared in low overhead. A few hands leaned listlessly over their rails watching the port fall away behind them, but most of the crews were below deck, busy with their jobs, preparing for what must soon come. Lamb watched them go, filled with a strange flat feeling, as if he were suddenly suspended between two worlds: the reality of the Cornish port and the unreality of the crazy, frightening landfall of the morrow. For what seemed a long time he stared at the black silhouettes steaming across the bleak grey sea towards the purple dusk already forming on the horizon. Then shaking himself, as if trying to awake from a dream, he went up to the bridge.

Doan and Degenhardt were waiting for him, eyes flashing back and forth as they watched the busy actions of the men on the deck. "Everything all right?" Lamb queried.

"Ay, ay, sir," the two men snapped together. "We've made a last check of the whalers and the depth-charge launchers," Doan added. "Both are okay."

"Fine."

Lamb looked across the deck at the earnest young commando officer who was presumably still lecturing his men on tactics. "Well, I hope we never have to use Rose Force, Number One," he mused aloud. "But I'm afraid we might have to. That Wall-Jones is keen, all right, but he's awfully green."

Doan nodded agreement, but said nothing.

Lamb turned to Degenhardt. "What are you arming them with, Chief?" he asked.

"Side-arms, grenades, rifles, sir. And I managed to wangle a couple of brens and a Yankee tommy-gun — for myself, sir." He grinned suddenly, showing a mouthful of sawn-off, dingy-yellow teeth.

Lamb grinned too, but as he did so, he wondered what it must feel like for the old petty officer to be going into action against his own people again; for CPO Degenhardt had once been a member of the German Navy until a run-in with a member of the Nazi Brown Shirts had forced him to flee Germany and eventually join the Royal Navy.

But if Degenhardt had any inhibitions left about fighting his own nation after three years of active service on the *Rose,* he did not show them. His wizened dark face was as contained and businesslike as always.

Lamb took one last look around the deck. All was purposeful activity. Even Wide Boy Stevens, whom Lamb suspected was not particularly keen on the *Rose* and her mission, was rubbing away at the firing pin of the breech-block with an oily rag, under Scouse's supervision, as if his very life depended on it. For all the faces of the crew revealed, they might well have been setting out on some dreary, routine patrol. Lamb smiled, confident that the crew, new hands and old hands alike, wouldn't let him or HMS *Rose* down.

He swung round on a waiting Doan. "Fo'c'sle secured for sea, Number One?" he demanded.

"Ay, ay, sir!" Doan responded smartly.

"All right, Number One, she's yours ..."

Two hours later they were out of the estuary and beginning to hit the first heavy water. On the little bridge, Commander Lamb began to feel the harsh sea air biting his face. He buried his face deeper into the rough, hairy collar of his duffle-coat. Somewhere in the growing purple gloom to his front was the rest of the attack force. But Lamb accepted being "tail-end Charlie". It was a role that HMS *Rose* had played often enough in these last three years; he was used to it.

Yet in spite of the lowly task which had been assigned to the *Rose,* Lt-Commander John Lamb could not quite control the heady excitement which overcame him at that moment and made him shudder with an almost sexual thrill. The *Rose* was sailing into action again, and beyond that purple horizon, each man of her crew would soon be confronted by his own personal destiny.

Behind the lean grey destroyer, her wake now being whipped into frothy white cream as she gathered speed, the coast of England started to slip away into the darkness, leaving the *Rose* alone with the green, heaving sea and the unknown dangers which lay ahead of her ...

# Operation Chariot

# *ONE*

"Unidentified object off the port bow!" the lookout sang out suddenly.

On the bridge of the *Tynedale,* Commander Ryder, Colonel Newman and the *Tynedale's* navigating officer Lt Green swung up their binoculars.

It was the afternoon of their second day out and up to now the little convoy of destroyers and supporting motor launches had encountered nothing more serious than a heavy swell, which had caused havoc once more with the commandos' sensitive stomachs. Did this unidentified object signify that they had run into trouble at last? Hastily the square-jawed naval force commander adjusted his binoculars until he had the ship to their port in full focus.

"Dammit!" he cursed, knowing instinctively that there could be no mistake. "It's a Jerry U-boat!"

Almost immediately there was controlled chaos. Suddenly sailors were running back and forth along the slick wet deck, sirens were howling, and down in fire control the young, excited sub was crying: "Bearing green three-oh ... range one thousand ... deflection — zero. *FIRE!"*

The destroyer's 4.5-inch guns opened up with a crash. An instant later, the new Swiss Oerlikon cannon followed suit. In a frantic chatter, the 20 mm shells chased across the green water, drawing a glowing red and white trail behind them. Gleaming yellow, steaming shell cases tumbled to the deck in crazy profusion. Great spouts of water shot into the grey sky all around the submarine. But still not one shell struck her.

On the bridge, Commander Ryder struck the bulkhead with his fist and cried, "Come on, come on, sink the bugger!"

But they were to be denied the pleasure. As the German U-boat became aware of the danger in which she found herself, tiny black figures ran the length of her narrow deck and scrambled frantically up the ladder to the conning tower. The *Tynedale's* gunners renewed their efforts, aware that the Jerry would escape in another minute. But their aim was too excited, too erratic. The last German sailor threw himself inside the hatch. White water bubbled the length of the U-boat's bow. The bow inclined at a steep angle and Ryder realized despairingly that the Jerry was crash-diving. She was getting away.

*"CEASE FIRE!"* he yelled into the speaking tube above the clatter and chatter of the Oerlikons, *"PREPARE TO DEPTH CHARGE!"*

Together the two Hunt class destroyers surged forward at thirty knots, a great white bone in their teeth, as they left the *Campbelltown* behind. In two wild, yet graceful curves, sending up twin wings of flying water behind them, they came in for the depth charge attack. At the bows of both ships, there was a succession of soft plops. Dark clumsy objects — the depth charges — shot high into the air then fell into the water in the creamy wakes. For what seemed a long time, nothing happened.

Suddenly the water erupted. Great spouts shot into the air.

On the crazily shaking bridge of the *Tynedale,* Commander Ryder focused his glasses urgently. But what he expected to see did not materialize — the black sleek bow of the U-boat coming up and breaking the surface at an impossible angle. Had the depth charges missed?

"Bring her about," he yelled at the coxswain who had taken over the wheel from the leading hand, "let's go and have a look-see!"

"Ay, ay, sir," the petty officer sang out.

He swung the wheel around with a will, knowing as well as the captain, how vital it was for the whole operation, to know whether they had sunk the sub or not.

While the *Atherstone* took up a covering position, her 4.5 inchers trained on the water near the *Tynedale,* her sister ship, now slowed down to ten knots. It was a highly dangerous thing to do, Ryder knew. If the sub had not been sunk by the depth charge attack, the Hunt class destroyer was an open invitation for a torpedo at that speed. But Ryder also knew it was a chance he had to take.

Slowly the *Tynedale* steamed down the path of the depth charge attack, look-outs searching the water on both sides of the ship, eyes anxious and strained. On the bridge Commander Ryder was no less worried. Carefully, systematically, he swept his binoculars from side to side, seeking desperately for the signs that would tell him that the depth-charge attack had succeeded — the oil traces, the bits and pieces of naval flotsam, the slow-bursting bubbles of trapped air, the bodies.

But there was nothing. Not even the sudden flood of excess oil to the surface or packed bundle of naval cast-offs, which would indicate that the sub-commander, an old hand at this deadly cat-and-mouse game, was releasing oil or firing a hastily collected bunch of the crew's spare duds through the torpedo tubes to simulate a sunken U-boat. *Nothing!*

Twice the *Tynedale* traced and re-traced the pattern of the depth charge attack without result, and as the *Campbelltown* and the motor launches started to catch up with the two almost stationary Hunt class destroyers, Commander Ryder was finally forced to abandon the search.

"Well, Commander?" Colonel Newman asked, as Ryder, his face creased by a worried frown, leaned against the chart table, watched by an equally anxious Lt Green. "What do you think? Did you get him?"

"I don't know, Colonel. I bloody well don't know! There is no trace that we sank the bugger and there is no trace — the usual dodges U-boat skippers pull — that he isn't down there, fifty fathoms below us at this moment, thanking his lucky stars that he's got away with it."

Colonel Newman hesitated a moment before he put the vital question. While they were at sea, Ryder, although he was the junior officer, was in charge of the *whole* force. It was up to him to make the decision and at that particular moment, Colonel Newman was very glad that it was so. "Well, Ryder, what are we going to do?" He stopped abruptly. He had said enough. Ryder would know what he meant.

Indeed, Lt-Commander Ryder knew well enough what the commando Colonel's question implied. If the sub were still unsunk, it would undoubtedly radio the sighting of the assault force to the German Naval High Command HQ at Kiel and within seconds of the receipt of that signal, the alert warnings would be flashing out to every German base along the whole French coast. And that would mean the Jerries would be waiting for them. Operation Chariot would end in a massacre!

Ryder licked his dry lips, while the other two officers stared at him wide-eyed and strained, knowing all too well just what mental agony their Commander must be enduring at that particular moment. Yet if they had sunk the Jerry U-boat and he called off the operation by mistake, what would be the reaction at home? Their Lordships would hush up the whole business, of course. After the *Gneisnau-Scharnhorst* fiasco, they could not afford to have another scandal affecting the Royal Navy.

A sudden, alarming thought shot through Ryder's mind. But what if the *Tirpitz* did break loose, as Mountbatten predicted she would if St Nazaire was not closed to her? He could well imagine the destruction and chaos she would cause with half the Home Fleet chasing her and the merchantmen on the Atlantic run left defenceless and wide-open to the killer U-boat packs. Things were bad enough at home with the civvies down to two ounces of meat a week and one "real" egg, as they were now calling it, a month. If the vital food supplies from America didn't get through for even as little as a couple of weeks, it might be the last straw which broke the camel's back. The civvies couldn't stand much more.

Commander Ryder swung his gaze to the bobbing motor launches and their khaki-clad cargo. If he made the wrong decision now, he knew he could be condemning every last one of them to death. It was a tremendous responsibility.

"Well, Commander?" Newman said softly, unable to bear the tension of waiting any longer.

"We go on, Colonel," Ryder said, his voice controlled and completely devoid of emotion.

"Good show!" Colonel Newman said with fake heartiness. "Jolly good show, Commander."

Swiftly the convoy began to gather speed again. France was only two hours away now.

With a hand that trembled violently, Leutnant Dietz, captain of the U-102, wiped the sweat off his dripping brow, and breathed, "Holy straw sack, that was a damn near thing, Fritz."

His second-in-command Fritz Haberkamp nodded, not trusting himself to speak, his ears still filled with the frightening roar of the depth charges and the ear-splitting, bone-shaking chaos, the lunatic confusion of crashing glass and cursing, frightened crewmen, which had followed.

"Emergency lighting!" Dietz ordered.

The boat flooded with a weak yellow light from the emergency generators. Carefully the Captain stepped over the littered deck and tapped the pressure meter. The luminous green needle swung up above the red mark. It looked all right. They hadn't been holed after all. He swung round. "Report your damage," he ordered softly, as if the British destroyers might still be somewhere above him.

One by one the soft replies flashed back to the control centre.

Dietz smiled his thanks. "Look-out," he commanded, raising his voice now, more confidently, "what did you see before they spotted us?"

The skinny, bearded petty officer snapped to attention. "Destroyers — three of them, captain!"

"That all?"

"Yessir. Certain sir," the *Obermaat* replied.

"Good." Dietz made a decision. "We'll break radio silence. Signal *OKM*\* Kiel. Three enemy destroyers sighted sixteen hundred hours, steering course for La Pallice."

\* German Navy HQ.

As the radio operator bent over his morse key, Haberkamp broke his silence and asked in a voice which was still not quite steady, "What do you think they're up to, skipper?"

Dietz shrugged. "Search me, Fritz. We'll leave that to the gentlemen in Kiel with all the gold lace to figure out ..."

# TWO

At exactly ten o'clock on the night of March 27th, 1942, Lt Green, in charge of the assault force's navigation, spotted the light winking suddenly out of the moonlit darkness. Immediately he had the Captain called to the bridge and pointed out the winking light to him. "It's the *Sturgeon,* sir," he explained.

Swiftly Ryder focused his night glasses. He could just make out the long grey shape of HM Submarine *Sturgeon,* which had been ordered by Mountbatten to act as a signal beacon off the mouth of the River Loire.

The Captain dropped his glasses to his chest and swung round to Green, a happy smile on his freshly shaven face. "Congratulations, Green," he cried. "Dead on time and in exactly the right place. A fine job of navigation."

Green blushed, happily.

A few moments later *Sturgeon,* her job done now, signalled good-bye and good luck and disappeared beneath the waves once more.

Now all was haste. As the assault force hove to, Colonel Newman quickly shook hands with Commander Ryder, then with the rest of his staff transferred to *Motor Gun Boat 314.* Once the balloon went up, the staff would land on shore to supervise the secondary operation; the demolition of the submarine pens and as much else of the German harbour installations as could be managed in the one and half hours allotted to the assault force. Swiftly, as the two Hunt class destroyers prepared to stand off the mouth of the Loire, the ships formed up once again, in battle order. *Motor Gun Boat 314* was in the lead now, with Lt Commander Beattie's *Campbelltown* which now flew the black cross and swastika of the German *Kriegsmarine,* following close behind and escorted on both sides by the launches carrying the commandos. *Motor Torpedo Boat* 74 brought up the rear.

On the *MGB 314,* the young skipper rapped out an order. The little ship started to draw away. Behind it, the *Campbelltown* followed suit. In the little launches, the pale-faced commandos, nearly three hundred of them, grabbed the sides hastily as the craft began to move once more.

Up on the *Atherstone's* bridge, Commander Ryder breathed out a sigh of relief. He must have sunk the German U-boat. They were almost in position now and no alarm had been sounded. Now for the time being, his part in Operation Chariot was over. "Signaller," he cried.

"Ay, ay, sir."

"Make a signal to *Motor Gun Boat 314, to* Colonel Newman." The signaller hunched over the Aldis lamp.

Ryder smiled suddenly. *Tynedale* was after all, the commandos' parent ship. The signal might help to break the tension. "All right, signaller, here goes. Signal ... *'Do not forget whose father am I'.*"

A moment later, the white light blinked across the water from the MGB. *"I won't,"* it read, *"dear Daddy ..."*

Ryder laughed.


A high silver moon hung in the sky, casting a pale spectral light on the estuary. Now the wind had died away to a light breeze and the assault ships hissed softly through the dark cold swell. Now the only sounds which disturbed the night were the throb of the ships' engines and the drone of the RAF bombing force overhead, flying towards St Nazaire to carry out the diversion, aimed at covering their approach.

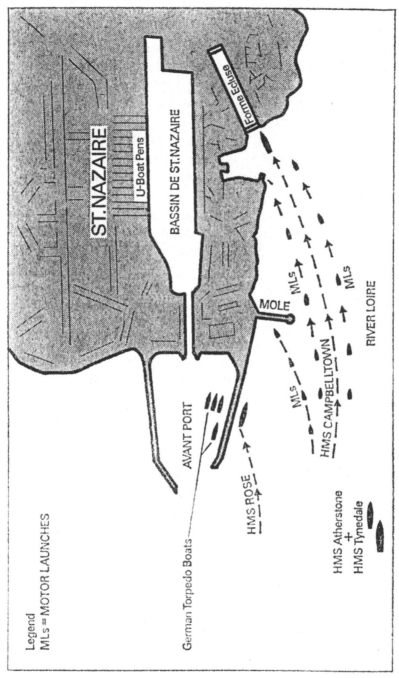

Legend
MLs = MOTOR LAUNCHES

THE ASSAULT FROM THE SEA (March 28th, 1942)

Suddenly two white fringes like low cloud emerged from the silver gloom on both sides of the assault force. Colonel Newman on the bridge of the motor gunboat started, but the young skipper next to him laughed softly and said, "Not to worry, sir. It's just the surf. We're entering the mouth of the river now."

"Oh, I see. Thank you for the info."

The force passed on, bunching up a little, as the river began to narrow. Up ahead, the RAF bombers were starting their raid. Abruptly, searchlights poked white fingers of icy light into the sky, parting the clouds in the search for the intruders. Red and white tracer zipped upwards angrily. Newman flashed a look at his wrist-watch. It was eleven hundred hours exactly. The RAF was dead on time, and everything seemed to be running well. So far there hadn't been a single hitch.

The minutes passed. The sudden white wash of water on both sides of the ships indicated that they were approaching the mudflats which they had been warned about at the final briefing. The young skipper of the motor gun boat ordered speed reduced. Carefully the *MGB 314* passed over the obstruction. The skipper flung an anxious glance behind him. Now it was the *Campbelltown's* turn, and her displacement was six times that of the gunboat. Would she make it? If the destroyer got stuck on the flats, that would be the end of the whole bold operation.

Suddenly he caught his breath. The *Campbelltown* had shuddered visibly! Still she kept on coming, her speed reduced to about ten knots now. She struck the mudflats again. But they couldn't stop her. An instant later she was picking up speed again, followed by her attendant motor launches, having cleared the flats by a matter of inches. Now there was nothing to stop them but the Germans ...

The searchlights blinded them! On the bridge of the MGB the skipper shaded his eyes against the glaring light blazing at them from both banks, seemingly only a matter of yards away and tensed in anticipation of the shells that *must* come. But he had not reckoned with Commander Beattie's ruse.

Leading Signalman Pike, wearing the uniform of a German petty officer, eyes narrowed to a squint against the glare, sprang into action. "Wait, do not open fire!" he signalled urgently and added the call sign of a German torpedo boat, which had been captured at the Vaagso raid. Then warming to his work, Pike sent a signal in plain language stating that two craft damaged by enemy action, requested permission to proceed to harbour without delay.

The ruse worked. Suddenly the lights went out and the force was able to sail on through the now total darkness. On the bridge of *Campbelltown,* Commander Beattie mentally paid tribute to the idea of cutting off the tops of the old ship's funnels so that she resembled a German *Möwe* class torpedo boat. It had paid dividends and averted disaster.

Five minutes passed. The assault force was getting ever closer to its target. Soon the ships would be level with the German's heaviest guns along the Mole. Suddenly a violet light flashed alarmingly on the Loire's northern bank. A shell whistled harmlessly across the water, towing a fiery scarlet trail behind it. Using the ship's brightest signal light, *MGB 314* made the international sign for ships being fired on by friendly forces. As suddenly as it had started, the firing died away. Now they had six minutes to go before the *Campbelltown* would ram the dock gate.


It was 01.20. The leading ships had already passed the German heavy batteries. They were within sight of their target — the thirty-five foot thick lockgates to the *Forme Ecluse.* Now, Commander Beattie, tensed on the bridge of the overage destroyer knew that nothing but a lucky Jerry shell on the bridge or steering gear could stop the *Campbelltown.* She was going to do it!

The seconds slipped by. Beneath his feet the *Campbelltown's* deck started to quiver as she picked up speed. She had come a long way for this moment — twenty-odd years, service in the Atlantic and Pacific as the USS *Buchanan* and that final long haul across the Atlantic. The result of the deal between Roosevelt and Churchill in late 1940 which had nearly cost the US President his presidency. Now she had come to the end of the road. But she would escape the ignominy of the naval knackers yard Beattie told himself, as the first dim outline of the gate loomed up from the darkness. The old *Buchanan* would die in a burst of glory! He pulled the plug out of the speaking tube. "Stand by to —"

At that moment, a German battery to the ship's port opened up with a frightening crash. It was exactly 01.27. And this time they had been well and truly spotted.

"Haul down the Jerry flag!" Beattie yelled urgently, as the German batteries on both sides of the river started ranging in, in earnest.

A rating, outlined stark black against the brilliant white light which suddenly flooded the *Campbelltown,* in a curiously theatrical manner, doubled for the aft and ran down the black and white flag. As the first shells began to strike the overage destroyer, the sailor ran up the red and white of the White Ensign.

The proud flag, flying stiffly in the sudden wind, as the destroyer rapidly gathered speed, drew the whole weight of the German fire on the ship. She staggered repeatedly as shell after shell struck her and enemy tracer hissed towards her like a swarm of red-hot angry hornets.

*"FIRE!"* the ship's gunnery officer yelled above the racket. Her gunners opened fire with everything they had. A German guard ship, hit by both the *Campbelltown* and the wild fire of its own coastal batteries heeled over and slipped below the boiling water. Red flames leapt up everywhere. Now the officers on the bridge could see the outline of the jetties and warehouses, structures they had memorized during training for so many weeks.

Beattie yelled out a slight change in course. The old ship responded for the last time. Now she was taking water at midships badly and the whole of her upper deck was riddled with shell holes. The dead and dying lay everywhere in the bloody, metal shambles. But still she managed to pick up speed in answer to the bridge telegraph, as if determined not to be cheated of this last moment.

At eighteen knots, the bullet-riddled White Ensign streaming proudly behind her, she headed straight for the great concrete and metal dock gate. Immediately to her front a desperate German battery blazed away at point-blank range. Her deck disappeared, in a mass of smoke and flames. At their brens, the dying gunners lying among the wreckage fought till they dropped dead over their inadequate weapons. Still she kept on going. Now, nothing could stop her.

With a great crash, scarlet flames streaming from her, she rammed the gate at dead centre. At that speed she did not stop until her wrecked bridge was level with them. Then, rearing her bow into the air like a wild horse put to the saddle for the first time, a violent tremor ran through her. Her one remaining mast came tumbling down, dragging a crazy spaghetti of wires behind it. Down below, the water started to pour in making a terrifying sound.

It was exactly 1.33 p.m. HMS *Campbelltown* had destroyed the main gate to the *Forme Ecluse*. Laughing crazily, the survivors, Navy and Army, started to pour over her shattered sides, to tackle the German batteries. Operation Chariot was well and truly under way.

# THREE

"Five minutes to go!" Lt Doan bawled through the loudhailer. *"Five minutes,* you commandos!"

Lamb threw a quick glance to their front, as the *Rose* slowly approached the commandos' landing place. To the right, the shore was a spectacular scene of multi-coloured tracer with the sky already coloured an ominous deep pink. Ahead of them, however, the shoreline was still dark and untroubled. Obviously the *Rose's* approach had not yet been spotted by the enemy radar or the German coastal look-outs. So far, so good!

He turned again and stuck out his hand at Wall-Jones. "Well, Lieutenant, it looks as if this is *it,"* he said, faking a smile.

The young officer was very pale and his hand was sweaty in Lamb's, but he returned Lamb's pressure firmly enough. "Yessir. It does. I'd better be off."

"Yes. I'll come down and see you off."

Down on the deck all was ordered, if hectic activity. Under Doan and Degenhardt's direction, the hands were guiding the commandos into the four whalers and launches which would take them ashore for their assault landing, on the nearest jetty of the *Avant Port.* Now the hands were packing in the "brown jobs" (as they called them) like sardines, their weapons gripped between their knees as they crouched there, laden with sixty pounds of equipment.

Lamb looked at their pale faces. They looked very English and ordinary, not at all like the brutal image of the commandos that the Press presented to the country. They were ordinary men who had been called from the normal routine of peacetime existence, given uniforms, trained to fire their weapons, hardened, toughened — and then suddenly faced with the terrible deadly reality of this moment. Lamb felt very proud of being British at this moment, of being one with such men who were going to face their ordeal stoically, as if their fate had been decided upon long ago.

"Remember," Wall-Jones shouted above the noise, 'there'll be about two feet of water off the jetty when you jump, so be ready for it!"

"Don't forget the diver, sir. I'm going down now, sir," some wag answered, using the popular phrase from ITMA. There was a soft ripple of laughter from the others, game but unconvincing.

Wall-Jones smiled, and adjusting his absurd sword clambered into the lead whaler.

"Good luck — and happy landings!" Lamb shouted.

"Thank you, sir." Wall-Jones answered without looking back. The Navy had done their part; he was finished with them now. His gaze was directed to his front and the horror soon to come.

"All right," Doan cried through the loud-hailer, checking that the hands were present at the winches, "lower away boats there!" The operation had started.


Cautiously, so as not to overbalance, Wall-Jones raised himself to his knees, already soaked from the flying spume, and stared to his front. The high jetty was clearly outlined against the sky, its base marked by a white frill of waves. It looked peaceful and harmless. But he knew from Colonel Newman's briefing that its top was piled high with lines of dannen wire, and that there were at least half a dozen pill-boxes and sandbagged gun emplacements guarding the approach to the basin containing the four *Möwe* class torpedo boats.

Wall-Jones was afraid. But then all his life he had been afraid of one thing or another: afraid he wouldn't pass Common Entrance; afraid the other boys would make fun of his absurd middle-class name (for most of his school life he had been "Balls-Jones"); afraid he wouldn't get through WOSB to receive a commission (his mother had been appalled by the thought that he might remain an "otherranker"); afraid of his men, who seemed to come from another and easier world than his with their "fags" and "bints" and "jars"; afraid of "letting the Colonel down"; afraid of being afraid. Always in his eighteen years of life, there had been someone pushing him, forcing him to do things he was scared of doing. And now suddenly when he really needed support, he was alone: an inexperienced youngster, who still only shaved twice a week. He was responsible for the fates not only of his thirty commandos, but possibly of the whole assault force, once they had started their journey back downstream.

Wall-Jones swallowed hard and knew abruptly — with the clarity of a vision — that he was going to die this cold March morning in a country he had never seen till now. But all that mattered was that he didn't make a fool of himself. Suddenly he heard his own voice — and it sounded remarkably steady — order: "All right, men, stand by to land!"

Behind him, his commandos gripped their weapons tighter in hands suddenly slippery with sweat and began to chew their gum at a more rapid rate. Before them the jetty wall reared up into the sky, stark black and impossibly high, and they could hear the stony hiss of the gravel as the tide slid it back and forth at the base of the concrete.

Suddenly the lead whaler's keel rasped against underwater barbed wire. "Bollocks," the leading hand at the tiller cursed, 'that's sodding well torn it!"

The boat came to an abrupt halt.

"All out!" Wall-Jones yelled, feeling miraculously in control of himself. Flourishing his sword over his head — his father had taken it to France with him in 1914 — he dropped over the side into waist-deep water. His commandos followed automatically.

Behind him, as he started to struggle through the tug of the water across the treacherous sliding gravel under his boots, the Troop's wag hissed: "After you, Claude!"

"No, after you Cecil!" his mate replied loyally, using the ITMA patter, which covered up a lot of tense moments in the men's lives.

Swiftly, their weapons and explosives held high above their heads, the commandos left the trapped boat strung out in a long line and began to wade for the jetty. The others from the launches followed.

Wall-Jones paused at the bottom of the dripping, green, encrusted jetty wall. Its top seemed deserted, and as far as he could judge with the racket coming now from the *Forme Ecluse,* they had still not been spotted. "All right," he rapped, "Smith and Barnes — over here!"

The two commandos, wet to the waist, sprang to his side and automatically spread their legs to take the strain, while extending their clasped hands: Wall-Jones put his booted foot on them, and as they grunted with the effort levered himself up and clasped the wet, rough top of the wall. Behind, another commando was going through the same procedure — and another.

Wall-Jones took a deep breath and heaved. Now he was on the top, crouched low to present the smallest possible silhouette. He could see the long rows of wire in front of him and beyond them a low sand-bagged shape, which must be a bunker. He took in the situation in a flash. They would have to get through the wire without alarming the bunker. Once across the jetty and through the sheds on the other side, they'd be right in among the German torpedo boats. Naturally they'd be manned and there'd be sentries on their decks. But the sailors, untrained in land combat, would be no match for his commandos. But first they would have to get through the damned dannert wire.

"Cutters!" he whispered.

The men crouched on top of the sea wall went into instant action. In three pairs they wriggled forward to the first section of wire. Cautiously, the man without the cutters felt the cruel wire, not heeding the barbs digging deep into his palms, testing to see if there was an alarm device attached. When he was satisfied that there was none, lying on his back, he held a strand of wire taut in bleeding hands while his mate crawled above him and began to clip through it.

The first line of wire was cut through. And the second. Immediately behind the wire cutters, Wall-Jones watched the sandbagged bunker anxiously for some kind of reaction. But it remained silent, as if whoever manned it had opted out of the murder and mayhem taking place further up the coast, and told themselves that it was none of their business. They were nearly through now. Wall-Jones could see the warehouses on the other side, with their boarded-up windows, quite clearly. They were obviously unoccupied; they would present no danger. "Get ready to move fast," he whispered to the tense commandos, lining up behind him weapons at the ready. "Pass the word on — get ready to move!"

The leading pair of wire-cutters wriggled forward on their bellies to the final barrier between them and the warehouses. Wall-Jones' young heart began to beat faster. They had nearly done it. Perhaps he was not fated to die in this foreign country, whose only significance for him up to now had been irregular verbs and not forgetting the *"cedilla"* under the "C" in Besançon. Cautiously, the commando with the bleeding hands grasped the wire, preparatory to pulling it taut for the man with the clippers.

And then it happened! The soft dry crack of a small explosion, followed by the hush of a flare. Next instant they were blinded by the fiery red glare of the signal flare hanging directly above them, revealing them in all their tense-faced, frightened defencelessness.

"Bollocks," the Troop's wag cried, "a trap flare! Can I do you now, sir!"

The rest of the ITMA patter was drowned by the cries of alarm and fear coming from the suddenly alerted bunker.

*"Alarm ... Alarm ... Die Tommies sind da ... schnell, schnell, an die Waffen, Leute!"*

Barnes, the Troop's "old man" at 29, reacted instinctively. Raising himself to his full height, he swung back his arm, like a bowler in a village cricket match, and hurled a grenade at the bunker, just before the first wild burst of machine gun fire ripped his chest apart.

The grenade exploded in a vicious ball of yellow fire at the entrance to the bunker. The half-naked men running out of it came to an abrupt stop. Suddenly, torn bodies were flying everywhere. The machine gun stopped firing abruptly.

"At the double!" Wall-Jones yelled, his voice suddenly high and boyish:

The wire-cutter teams did not hesitate. One man flung himself on to the last line of wire, ignoring the cruel barbs piercing his flesh everywhere. His mate ran straight at him and sprang over the four foot high wire. Another soldier followed — and another.

*"Achtung, der Draht!"* an enraged voice shouted somewhere in the darkness. *"Die Tommies klettern ueber den Draht!"*

Rifle fire ripped the night apart. As Wall-Jones sprang over the prostrate man on the wire, the Commando screamed and suddenly went limp, while the others continued to run over his dead body.

They ran on desperately towards the warehouses, the volume of German fire mounting by the second. At the corner of the first one, Wall-Jones skidded to a stop. From somewhere came the sound of breaking glass, as if someone had smashed in a window with a rifle butt. Instinctively he knew what that meant. The Germans were breaking into the warehouses ahead of them, trying to block their way to the boats. But there was no time to hesitate. Behind him half his force was still trapped in the wire, lying flat on their bellies, fully exposed to the German fire from the bunker, but giving back as good as they got. With him were a mere ten men. But they would have to do.

"All right," he whispered, "no time for fancy tactics. Keep to each side of the road — and in the shadows. And keep moving fast till we get to the boats. Okay, let's move out — at the double!"

The handful of commandos needed no urging. Already the harsh, hysterical hiss of a Spandau was sending a stream of vicious tracer towards them, trying to find their hiding place in the shadows. They doubled.

Wall-Jones raised his sword and yelled an obscenity. Straight ahead he could just make out the sharp, rakish funnel of one of the German torpedo boats, rearing up above a shed. They were almost there. "Get those satchel charges —"

His order was drowned by the chatter of machine gun fire to their right. At his side a commando screamed as he was hit. He staggered and tried to continue. But another burst hit him and he dropped dead. "Oh, Gawd," the man to his right cried in anguish, as the same streak of red tracer slammed into his stomach and stopped him in his tracks. He shrieked and fell on his face.

Wall-Jones stumbled on. Now his force was down to five. A grenade exploded against the wall of the warehouse and the machine gun fire died away at once. They ran on. There was the dry crack of a sniper's rifle. Behind Wall-Jones, Berry, the Troop's wag, stopped in his tracks. Suddenly his knees began to give way beneath him — "Don't forget the diver, sir. Going down now ..." His last words were choked in a thick vomit of blood and torn lungs. He sank to the ground and drowned in his own rich blood.

Now they were four.

They clattered round a corner. A German, helmet missing, was standing there hesitantly, his bald head gleaming in the red glare of battle. Wall-Jones brought down his sword. Its sharp blade cleaved deep into the elderly soldier's skull. He screamed once and fell to the ground immediately. Wall-Jones stared down at him in horror. At school, even dissecting a frog in biology made him puke; now he had actually killed a man!

"Get a move on, sir!" someone behind him cried giving him a push in the back. "Yon bugger's had it for sure!"

He pulled out his sword — it made a nauseating, sucking sound — and ran on. A German stick grenade sailed through the air, trailing its tail of fiery sparks: It exploded harmlessly behind them, but the blast lent speed to their heels. There'd soon be plenty more where that came from

Another corner. Before them there stretched the sleek camouflaged length of the German torpedo boat, with sailors in their beribboned floppy hats running up and down its cluttered deck, obviously preparing to get her underway. The commandos didn't hesitate. They ran forward through the ragged, wild fire that was now coming towards them from the ship. Wall-Jones felt a momentary red-hot burning pain in his right knee. Next to him his commandos were throwing grenades to keep the ship's crew pinned down. They were exploding all along the ship's length. In a moment they would begin tossing their satchel charges at her. "Come on, lads!" Wall-Jones felt more confident than he'd ever done in his short life before, "we've got 'em by the short and curlies now!" He was pleased with the soldiers' phrase and had a brief vision of the pained disapproval his mother would have shown if she'd heard him. "Move in from the right —"

The blast of the quadruple 20 mm ship's cannon hit them at close range. The shells stopped them dead, as if they had run into a solid brick wall. One commando disappeared completely. Another's head rolled away like a bloody football. A third slapped to the cobbles, the clothes ripped from his torso to reveal a purple-blue mess of pulped flesh and bone.

Wall-Jones felt himself being lifted high into the air by the blast, then his body was slammed down hard on the bloody cobbles. He gasped for breath urgently, but felt no pain, as he lay there feeling the life slip away from him.

*"Feuer einlegen ... feuer einlegen!"* someone was shouting from far, far away in a hoarse bass.

The tremendous chatter of the flak cannon stopped. But it meant little to Wall-Jones, save for relief that the noise had stopped. Suddenly for the first time in his young life, he felt happy. He knew he was dying, but he had done his job without making a fool of himself — that was the important thing.

As the blood-red haze began to descend upon him, he had an abrupt vision of the school's 19th century pseudo-gothic chapel, all stained glass and pointed grey arches, and Blake's *Jerusalem* as the school hymn. He remembered the faded oak of the board with its gilt-written names of the old boys who had died for "King and Country". His father's name had gone up there in 1924, the year of his birth, when the mustard gas from the Third Ypres had finally rotted away his lungs. He had died one sunny afternoon on the front lawn of their suburban villa. "Captain Terence Wall-Jones, MC, TD, KIA". Now soon his own name would appear on that board. Lt Terence Wall-Jones, undecorated, killed in action too, somewhere in France, 1942.

His mind moved on. "Where the bee fucks, there fuck I," they had sung in the back row of the school choir, mutilating Shakespeare's "Where the bee sucks, there suck I ..."

1939, was the year they had listened that Sunday to Chamberlain's words and he had felt somehow they had a special relevance to himself. At half-term, his mother had cried a lot — mysteriously. That year they had told the joke (endlessly) of Little Audrey seeing Mr and Mrs Wong wheeling their white baby in a pram and laughing and laughing because "she knew very well that two Wongs don't make a white".

He laughed hoarsely at the joke. Blood welled up inside, flooding his lungs, hot, salty and vaguely unpleasant. One moment before the big, nailed sea boot thudded into his shattered ribs and the voice in German cried *'tot'',* he died, Lt Terence Wall-Jones, Second Commando, aged 18 ...

# FOUR

From his vantage point on the bridge of HMS *Rose,* a horrified Commander Lamb could see everything in the alternating flash and blank darkness of the battle on the jetty: Within fifteen minutes he knew that the commandos had failed to take their objective. The German torpedo boats were still not destroyed. The operation had been total failure.

Now the pitiful handful of survivors were coming aboard again in the sole remaining launch, hauled up by a solemn-faced group of hands under Degenhardt's command, who had dropped the usual good-humoured naval heckle at the expense of the "brown jobs": All were wounded and shocked to a terrible degree, their eyes wide and staring, bodies shaking and heaving as if with tropical fever.

Lamb watched them go down below. A youngster with curly hair, his mouth set in a look of reproach, as he dragged his bloody, naked leg behind him; another, ginger-haired and helmet-less, hopping cheerfully on one leg, puffing away on a "coffin nail"; a third, rolling his head from side to side, mumbling all the time, "it was a cock-up from the ruddy start ... a cock-up from the ruddy start ..: *a cock-up!"*

Lamb moistened his lips and cried above the roar of fire from the shore, "Chief, get the sick-bay attendants working on these men at once! See they have blankets and a drop of rum!"

"Ay, ay, sir," Degenhardt said and began to bellow out orders. "And report immediately you've seen to them!"

"Ay, ay, sir!"

Lamb turned to Doan, who had appeared from nowhere. "Number One!"

"Sir?"

"Stand by with Rose Force."

Doan responded immediately, putting his loud-hailer to his lips and yelling, "Fall in Rose Force — *at the double!*" The command boomed back and forth across the ship and those members of the crew who had been allotted to the emergency force for this eventuality before leaving England doubled forward to grab their weapons, which were already waiting for them on the blood-stained, littered deck, just vacated by the commando survivors.

Lamb swung round. Degenhardt was back on cue. "Chief, get your gunners out of "A" and "X" turrets and have 'em stand by at the Y-thrower, ready for action," he ordered.

By a sudden flash of scarlet flame from the jetty, where the Germans were still firing wildly at the piled-up heap of dead commandos, Lamb could see the grin on the petty officer's face. "What are you grinning like an ape for, Chief?" he demanded, curtly.

"Nothing, sir," Degenhardt answered smartly, his face disappearing into the gloom once again. "I just wanted to say I've already got the hands fell in."

So that was it. In spite of all his years in the Royal Navy where one did nothing unless ordered to do so, Degenhardt was still very much the thorough German, always prepared for the next move. "Good man, Degenhardt. All right, you know the drill?"

"Ay, ay, sir." Degenhardt snapped, very businesslike. "Once Mr Doan's party is away, we start to move in by the stern —"

"Yes, that way we'll present the smallest possible target to them, once they spot us and open fire."

Degenhardt carried on. "Then we open up with the depth charges as soon as we're in range."

"Yes, Chief, and make damn sure that you don't land any of 'em on the frog part of town! I don't want any other demands from their Lordships for compensation for sundry French houses destroyed on the morning of Saturday March 28th, 1942. They're still hounding me for a sextant I'm supposed to have lost as a sub in 1930!"

Don't worry, sir. I've got the two best men on the *Rose* on the job — Leading Seaman MacFadden and Able Seaman Stevens on the Y-thrower, personally."

"Those villains! All right, Chief, get on to it."

"Ay, ay, sir." Degenhardt doubled away.

Lamb turned back swiftly to Doan. "Now you're quite sure you know what to do, Number One?"

"Sure, skipper. After all, it was my idea back there in London, wasn't it?" Doan replied and Lamb could imagine him grinning in the darkness, though his face was only a vague blur.

Don't be so cocky, Doan. I'll see you get a medal for it."

"I've got a closet full of them already, sir. A nice pink gin would be more welcome at this particular moment, I guess."

"I'll have a bath-tub full of it waiting for you when you come back, Number One."

*"If"* Doan said to himself, but not to the skipper. That type of realistic pessimism was not subscribed to in the British Navy. At such moments one had to be all stiff upper-lip and three cheers for the red, white, and blue and all that. Instead he said: "Okay. For the record, sir. We swing out a little into the estuary and come in, in the centre of the harbour. The whaler's draught is so small that the anti-sub nets won't worry her — and it's my guess that the Krauts will have already raised the boom to let the torpedo boats get out and intercept our people."

"Agreed."

Doan continued. "From there we sail right up to main seawall — according to the briefing, the Krauts have no bunkers or pillboxes there — and work our way under the cover of your fire towards the torpedo boats."

"Right. At the most I can give you ten minutes, Doan," Lamb said, his voice worried. "I know you might be caught right out in the open without any protective fire at all. But I'm afraid I can't risk the *Rose* longer than ten minutes. By that time even the most nervous Jerry gunner will have us bracketed. Besides with a bit of luck those two rogues MacFadden and Stevens on the depth charge launcher might have done the job of destroying the torpedo boats for you."

"Maybe," Doan said easily and went on with the final phase of his plan. "Once the Krauts have had it, we double back to the whaler and head out the way we came in. We'll rendezvous off the entrance to the *Avant Port.*"

"Yes, Number One. I'll give you thirty minutes after you've fired your signal flare. After that I'm afraid we'll —"

"Have to make way," Doan finished the sentence for him. The overage destroyer, battered by twenty-odd years of unrewarding service was Lamb's life. For the *Rose,* Lamb would sacrifice everything and everybody, including himself. The American knew that and respected it. Lamb felt about his ship in a way that he knew he would never feel about one if he lived to be an admiral, which at the present moment he decided was hardly likely. "Don't worry about us, skipper," Doan said with forced cheerfulness. "I'll make it. You can't keep us Yanks down, you know."

"Of course, Number One. Now let's get this operation started."

A second later, strapping on the big .38, Doan was clattering down the companionway to his waiting command. The second attempt at destroying the E-boats had commenced.


Cautiously HMS *Rose* eased her way through the pink-grey gloom towards the jetty. Now the scarlet stab and thrust of gunfire had begun to die away, as the German defenders slowly realized that they had beaten off their surprise attackers from the sea. Standing tense and expectant on the bridge, his night glasses glued to his eyes, Lamb decided they had probably now found the commando dead — or had possibly even taken prisoners — and were congratulating themselves in their customary boisterous German way.

The Captain strained his eyes in an effort to penetrate the gloom, hoping against hope that the enemy wouldn't spot them before he could get within depth charge range, yet surprised that the Germans had not yet heard the steady throb-throb of the *Rose's* engines.

"Over there — to port, sir," the lookout sang out, in a subdued voice.

Lamb swung his glasses round.

Above the black, jagged silhouette of the port installations, he could make out the rakish funnels of the German E-boats. He recognized the *Möwe* class immediately and knew from Jane's *Fighting Ships* for 1941 that they were armed with two 21-inch torpedoes and two Oerilikon *Vierlingflak* cannon.* If they ever got to sea before the assault force left the estuary of the Loire they would play merry hell with the unarmed troop launches. He had to destroy them!

Ignoring the telegraph, he picked up the voice-tube and whistled through it. "Captain here," he said softly, as if the Germans on the shore, now only two hundred yards away, might conceivably hear him.

"Ay, ay, sir," the ER.9's thick Glaswegian burr came back up at him.

"Stop engines. We're going to drift in. But Chief, I want you ready to give me full power at once. Clear?"

"Ay, clear, sir. Dinna fash," he added with the authority of thirty years of service behind him, including three with the *Rose,* which he felt gave him a special relationship with the Captain, "yon engines'll no let ye down, sir."

"Of course, they won't, Chief."

Without looking round or taking his eyes off the jetty looming up ever larger to their front, he snapped at the leading hand on the wheel — a grey haired-stripey veteran —"Hold her steady! Nice and easy does it."

"Nice and easy does it, sir," the man replied, as unemotionally as if he were manoeuvring the *Rose* into Portsmouth harbour in peacetime, in broad daylight.

Slowly and silently, the little destroyer moved into position for attack.


A dry crack. A soft explosion. An instant later, the jetty — a mess of tangled wire, draped with the limp brown rags which were

* Quadruple Cannon

the commandos' bodies, and the startled German troops — was lit up by the cold yellow glare of a star shell: four slowly dropping lights being borne down by spinning small parachutes.

At the depth-charge launcher, Stevens and MacFadden tensed, while they waited for Degenhardt to give the signal to fire. Both of them knew how much depended on the accuracy of their aim and knew too, that the depth charge launcher had never been designed to act as a sort of primitive mortar, it would have to fire its bombs — depth charges — over a fifteen foot high jetty-wall, across a broad stretch of quay, then plank them down accurately on the Four German ships on the other side.

"Peanuts!" Wide Boy had snarled, when Scouse had asked him if he could do it five minutes before. "It's like taking candy off a kid," he had added, in his best gangster manner. Now he wasn't so sure. The damned jetty wall seemed very high and he wondered whether the depth charges would clear it.

"All right, dead-eye Dick," Scouse whispered, "get ready!"

Wide Boy didn't turn, but he could sense that Scouse's heart was beating as rapidly with tension as was his own. Hastily he wiped his sweating hands on his jumper and grasped the end of the lashed-in rope.

*"NOW!"* Degenhardt roared, knowing instinctively that the *Rose* dare not go in much further; she'd run aground.

Scouse's hand came down hard on Wide Boy's shoulder. *"FIRE!"* he yelled.

Wide Boy tugged hard. There was the crack of the explosive charge. The great drum of explosive went sailing slowly into the air, whirling round and round as it did so. Gradually, with maddening slowness, it gained height and then suddenly it had cleared the jetty wall and Scouse was yelling exuberantly, "fire the other one, you silly cockney sod! FIRE IT, I SAY!"

In a daze, Wide Boy tugged again.

He opened his mouth just in time to save his eardrums from being burst as the first depth charge exploded with a tremendous roar, followed by the second one an instant later, beyond the road. But their explosion was nothing to the one that succeeded it. It was a great, all-consuming noise that seemed to go on and on, lighting the whole front in its fierce, burning yellow flame which turned night to day and showed them the great gap in the warehouses, and beyond it the funnel of the first torpedo boat, hanging down at a crazy drunken angle.

"You've done it!" Scouse yelled excitedly. "You've done it, yer big streak of London piss!"

"Good work there, lad!" Degenhardt cried, no less excited.

And then the first German salvo, enraged and wildly off mark, hit the water in great spouts of white just in front of them, and the ship's engines were throbbing madly beneath the gunners' feet as the engineer gave the *Rose* full power, and she started back into the gloom from which she came. But at the launcher, two crazily laughing hands, sweat streaming down their faces from the exertion of moving the great drums of explosive, fired on, as if they would never stop again, while a delirious Wide Boy told himself he had never been so worked up in all his young life; this was better than taking a pony off some country mug at poker. Suddenly he realized he was beginning to like HMS *Rose* — like her very much. And on the bridge, as the little destroyer heeled and lurched with each new explosion, Commander Lamb knew that it was up to Doan now. The *Rose* had done her bit. She could do no more. Now it was the American's pigeon ...

# *FIVE*

It was now two thirty, nearly an hour since HMS *Campbelltown* had rammed the gate to the *Forme Ecluse,* and the secondary operation of the Plan was going badly. Colonel Newman had landed. He had intended to seize a bridgehead on shore to cut off the approaches to the dockyard area from the rest of the town, while his demolition parties blew up as many of the sub pens and other port installations as possible. It had failed.

The party under the Commando's Regimental Sergeant Major, which had been detailed to seize a command post for him, had never made it. Their launch had been sunk in the estuary by enemy gunfire. The RSM had struck out bravely for the shore, towing a carley float laden with the survivors. Almost at once the little craft was flooded by German searchlights. What happened next was inevitable. Every enemy machine gun in the area concentrated its fire on the trapped men. They were wiped out, dying in the bullet-riddled, blood-filled boat.

In the burning confusion of falling timbers, smoke, and scarlet flames, Colonel Newman tried to sort out the situation. But without success. He'd hardly managed to establish a rough-and-ready CP, when two 88s on top of the sub pens opened up on the place, pumping shell after shell at him.

Another commando sergeant-major volunteered to try to put the 88s out of action with his 2-inch mortar. With an obscene grunt, the pathetic little weapon went into action against the great guns, and astonishingly the first bomb landed right on top of one of the German gun crews. The artillerymen went flying over the side of the concrete bunker like swatted flies. The second bomb was equally successful. It landed at the base of the other gun and exploded under it. An instant later, the long barrel drooped in submission. The CP was safe for a little while longer.

Now for a while, the commandos, hurrying to their objectives through the leaping flames, had some success. An assault party blew the steel door off the pumping station and racing down the steel stairs, planted their charges forty feet below the surface. In a flash they were on the outside again, lying flat on the ground while the white tracer zigzagged hectically just above their helmeted heads.

The explosives went off in a mad roar making the ground tremble wildly beneath them. With legs that felt like rubber, they staggered back the way they had come to check the results of their work. The pumping station was not completely destroyed, but seizing nearby sledge hammers, they began like a bunch of crazy navvies to wreck the surviving electric motors.

Another party, trapped on the Old Mole after destroying its German guns there, ran full-tilt into another German cannon, covering the iron-grid bridge which they must cross if they were to link up with the rest of the Commando. It was a desperate situation for which they had trained repeatedly these last two years. Their officer hesitated only a moment. "Over the side," he ordered above the vicious crackle of small arms fire and the persistent frightening boom of the enemy cannon which held them up. "At the double now, you, men!"

The commandos needed no urging. As one, they swung themselves over the side of the bridge, keeping low in order to diminish the target, and swinging from girder to girder like a bunch of monkeys, their booted feet nearly touching the water below, they made their way safely to the other side. A second later they had disappeared into the maze of shattered waterside buildings.

But by now fate was beginning to catch up with the burly Commando Colonel, armed only with a revolver and a stout ashplant. His force of nearly three hundred commandos was down to exactly seventy men — and half of them were wounded. Crouched in the ruins of his emergency CP, he yelled above the tremendous din outside, "this is where we walk home, lads. All the boats have been blown up — or have gone back."

Immediately there was a burst of excited suggestions from the survivors, not one of whom wanted to surrender. "What about going down to the quayside and swimming up-stream till we're clear of the ferries? ... How about trying to pinch one of their tugs, sir and running her down river? ... We could break east, right into 'em — they wouldn't expect that. With a bit of the old commando bash-on spirit, we'd be through 'em like a dose of salts before they knew what had hit 'em ...?"

But Newman was adamant. "No, lads, we're going to do it like this. We're going to break up into small parties — threes and fours, each one with an officer or NCO leading — and we'll make south for the Spanish frontier. You're not to surrender if you bump into old Jerry until all your ammo's gone." He smiled at them suddenly — those familiar, bloody, unshaven faces which he had known for two long years and which were somehow closer to him at this particular moment than those of his family — and said: "It's a lovely moonlight night for it."

Those words were the beginning of the end for Number Two Commando.


Captain Roy, in charge of the assault party, led the breakout. They reached the southern bank of the Bassin de St Nazaire without difficulty. Then the Germans spotted them. Roy's second-in-command went down with a bullet through his right knee. His men carried him for a little way in spite of the ever increasing enemy fire, then he ordered them — almost gaily — to leave him behind.

Now the Germans were massing on both sides of the narrow alleys the commandos must take if they wished to escape the trap they found themselves in, settling behind their Schmeissers and Spandau's on the roofs of the warehouses, waiting for the English to walk directly into their murderous fire.

And in due course, the English did walk into it, boldly, bravely, knowingly, firing from side to side like crazy men, whooping and yelling obscenities to each other and the enemy as they did so. Germans began to drop off the roofs like logs bouncing off bloody, littered *pavé* below before sprawling out grotesquely in death.

But all the time the commandos' numbers were getting ever smaller. They left the lanes, pushing through gardens, jumping over walls, climbing across roofs, trampling through cold frames, trying to escape that terrible German fire. To no avail. They dwindled by the minute.

A six-wheeled German armoured car, its turret buttoned down, rattled up an alley, spitting fire. Both German and British fell as its machine guns scythed the street before it. The commandos dodged down another passage and the situation became even more confused. A German motor-cycle complete with side-car came roaring up towards them. A commando knelt in the middle of the passage and let the enemy have a full burst with his tommy gun. The driver was catapulted from his seat, and the side-car smashed into a lamp-post, the passenger slumped forward, his face thrust through the broken glass, his neck broken. The commandos doubled on. But now time was running out fast for the survivors. They found a cellar, complete with dirty, lice-ridden mattresses. *"Lu f tschutrybunker,"* someone read the white-painted sign out hesitantly. "A Jerry air-raid shelter, sir."

Newman nodded wearily, feeling suddenly too old for this sort of thing after all. "Bed the wounded down on the mattresses," he commanded with a gasp. "We'll try to hide out here till nightfall and then we'll make for the open country in pairs." Their luck failed. A few minutes later, the door above them was kicked open brutally. A gruff voice commanded *"Raus da .. raus, sage ich!"*

Newman hesitated for only a fraction of a second. He knew he was beaten. One single potato-masher down those stairs would see the lot of them off, the wounded and the unwounded alike. "All right," he yelled, his voice defeated, "we surrender!"

Slowly the commandos, the unwounded helping their bleeding crippled mates, began to file up the stairs towards the waiting Germans.

Now the motor launches started to pull away. The German fire intensified. The water burnt with the hiss of tracer, coming in from both sides of the estuary. Motor Launch No. I blew up just south of the Old Mole. No. 262 received a direct hit in midstream and the survivors flung themselves overboard into the scarlet, glowing water to take their chances there. No. 268 was struck a great blow by a German shell. She reeled crazily. An instant later she exploded. There were no survivors. And so it went on — the massacre of the launches — until finally there were only three left, Nos. 270, 156, 446, their decks littered with the debris of battle and slick with blood, covered by the Motor Gun Boat. Now they started back down the river to the rendezvous with the two destroyers and what must await them there, if Lieutenant Doan, ex-US Navy, did not succeed in finishing off the remaining three German E-boats in the next sixty minutes.

# SIX

"Take it easy now, fellers," Doan whispered cautiously, as the whaler neared the entrance to the *Avant Porte,* with its two claws of sea-walls only a hundred and fifty yards apart at this particular point. "We're coming in now."

The men manning the oars needed no urging. As if walking over eggs, they wielded their oars with extreme care, hardly daring to dip the surface of the water, in case they hit some obstruction which could alarm the enemy on both sides of them. In the bow, his finger curled around the Force's only other tommy-gun, Doan hurled a silent prayer to heaven that they might get through without being observed. Yard by yard they slipped through the twin claws. No enraged call. No surprised challenge. Nothing. They were doing it!

Doan swallowed hard. "Pull away now!" he ordered.

The men took up the strain once again, putting their backs into it, as if they couldn't put enough distance between them and the bottle-neck of the harbour entrance. The whaler shot forward, as the harbour opened up to port and starboard and revealed the stark silhouettes of the various ships against the flames of the burning installations everywhere. In a matter of moments they were submerged into the confused maritime jungle of a busy port.

At the tiller, the petty officer in charge swung the whaler round, dodging between a rusting freighter and what looked like a German mine-sweeper — to judge by the winches on both her sides — and aimed the boat towards the centre of the harbour wall.

"Good man!" Doan cried. "That's the ticket!" ... "Slow ahead now, men," he ordered a moment later as a dark shadow high above them, a possible look-out, moved against the skyline on the freighter. "Duck!"

The men, veterans and new hands, ducked as one at his command. Silently, still propelled by the last powerful stroke of the oarsmen, the whaler swept by, and when Doan looked up cautiously a moment later the dark outline had vanished.

"Phew," he sighed, "thought we'd had it for a minute there, lads."

"And you know what thought did, sir," someone answered him. "He thought he shat hissen, he did."

There was a low rumble of laughter among the crew — a laughter in which Doan joined, knowing instinctively and joyfully that he could trust these men, who called him "Jimmy the One", "Our Yank" or worse things behind his back. They wouldn't let him down, although half the time he couldn't understand what they were saying when they lapsed into their regional dialects.

Slowly they neared the sea-wall. Doan could now smell that peculiar odour of all sea-walls he had ever known from Annapolis to Aberdeen: a compound of tar, seaweed, stale fish, diesel and something which he could only describe to himself as 'the sea and boots'. "All right, fellers," he whispered just before the old petty officer at the tiller beat him to it, "pull in your oars — we're here."

The whaler glided in these last few yards and nudged to a gentle stop against the barnacle-rough sea wall, while the rowers reefed their oars. "Sir," the man next to him whispered urgently, "there's a ladder just over here. I can feel it."

"Where?"

"Here, sir."

Doan reached out a hand, guided by the rating and felt the rough, flaky surface of a rusting sea-wall ladder. It was a bit of luck. It was going to make it much easier than he had anticipated. "Tie her up here, P.O." he ordered. "Here we go. After me at ten second intervals. Spread out and hit the deck as soon as you get top-side and woe-betide anybody who slips on the ladder or drops his weapon into the drink. You'll be on the rattle before you know what hits you."

In spite of the sudden knowledge of what they were now heading for, there was a subdued laugh at that: officers never used words like "rattle", or at least, British officers didn't. "Good old Yank", someone whispered.

But Doan no longer heard, he was already swinging himself up the rusting iron ladder using his left hand, the unslung tommy gun, ready for action in his right.

Gasping for breath, Doan paused at the last rung of the ladder, then gulping in air, he edged himself over the top and lay there on the wet concrete, absolutely still, smelling the stench of spilled diesel fuel only inches from his nostrils.

To his right, St Nazaire — or part of it — was burning merrily. To his left all was stillness and darkness. But to his front, he could make out mysterious figures and hear strange sounds in the pink gloom. He cocked his head to one side in order to hear better and could make out both French and German: the complaints of civilians doing that which they had been forced to do, and the angrier, more guttural grunts of German soldiers and seamen forcing them to do it.

He guessed the krauts were moving out French civilians or port workers — perhaps longshore-men — under guard. Just the confused situation he needed in order to get close to the kraut E-boats. He squirmed around and bending over the sea-wall, muffling his voice, he ordered: "Okay, come on."

The sailors raced up the iron ladder with professional ease and crouching on their haunches, grouped around him. "All right, lads, this is the way we're going to do it. First of all, get rid of those steel helmets of yours. They're a give away, that's for sure."

For a moment the hands hesitated, puzzled by the strange order until the petty officer commanded in a low bark. "Yer heard the officer, didn't yer? Get rid of them tin hats — at the double."

"Okay," Doan continued when they had removed them, "the Krauts'll take us for their own sailors in this confusion without the helmets. In a minute we're gonna form fours and *march* over to the torpedo boats." He chuckled at the boldness of his approach to the problem of getting close to the E-boats without being stopped or challenged, "and we're gonna whistle as we march — the Krauts always sing or whistle when they march. It's part of their training."

"But what we gonna whistle, sir?" the petty officer objected. "The hands don't know no Nazi songs."

Suddenly Doan recollected the pleasant little polka which had been all the rage in Hamburg in '36 when he had visited the port on a courtesy cruise with old USS *Quincy*. The thing had been called *"Rosamunde"* or something, until some cunning English song-writer had changed the words and made it the foremost marching song of the British Army. "Sing?" he exclaimed. "We'll sing *"Roll Out the Barrel"* — whistle that is. All right, form up!"

Whistling heartily and seemingly oblivious to the flames and noisy cries to their left, Rose Force marched crisply along the sea-wall in the direction of the E-boats, with Doan stepping out smartly in front, but with his trigger finger curled around the tommy-gun's trigger — just in case.

Once they were challenged, but Doan pretended not to hear. The challenger, hidden in the gloom, mumbled something which sounded like an apology and let them pass.

At last they were there. Doan could hear the throb of powerful diesel engines impatient to be off and suddenly in the blue flicker of dying flames, he could see the wrecked superstructure of the E-boat closest to the jetty, with the crew attempting to beat out the flames with shovels and blankets. "Halt!" he ordered swiftly, "and fall out."

"At the double!" the big petty-officer added his voice to the officer's.

They scattered hastily behind a pile of ammunition boxes stacked conveniently against the side of the sea-wall, while Doan, crouched low, took in the scene below. Degenhardt's depth-charges had badly damaged one of the E-boats and the ship next to her was silent as if she had been hit too, probably below the water-line. But the other two were undamaged, and by the throbbing of their engines and the purposeful activities of their crews outlined by the flames from the wrecked ship, Doan realized grimly that it would be only a matter of minutes before they slipped their cables and left. He had to act quickly.

Swiftly he scuttled back to the rest of his twenty-man force crouching behind the packing cases of ammunition. "Okay, this is the deal, fellers. We don't have time for anything fancy. From here on in, it's going to be hit-and-run. Petty Officer, you'll take half the men and spread out among these cases and cover me."

"Sir." The burly stoker petty-officer spread his arms out. "All right, all of you in front of me, grab yer bondhooks and move it."

They "moved it", spreading out swiftly among the cases, and forming a defensive semi-circle. Doan nodded approvingly; at least, his rear would be covered. He turned back to the remaining ten hands. "Okay, this is what we're going to do." He opened the haversack he'd slung over his shoulder and the night air was suddenly full of the heavy, bitter odour of almonds. "Plastic explosive," he explained, taking out the first, dark-brown putty-type block and handing it to the man nearest to him, "each one weighing about three pounds. The first five of you will get two of these blocks to plant at any good spot on those two boats down there, while the other five of you will cover your mates — you'll work in pairs. Understood."

"Ay, ay, sir," they all replied and one of them queried. "But how do we make it go off? Never had any dealing with this kind of stuff like, yer see, sir."

"I'm not surprised. It was on the secret list until last month." Doan said and produced what looked like a brass pencil. "A *time pencil.* Once you've found your spot to plant the stuff, stick this thing into it and pull the catch." He demonstrated how easily the pencil, which was a detonator, went into the soft material of the explosive. "It'll give us five minutes to get clear before the balloon goes up — at least, I *hope* the boffins who set them did their sums right, and have given us a full five!" He forced a grin. "If they haven't — well we'd better not talk about that. Okay, everybody clear what he's got to do?"

"Yessir," they answered as one.

"Right, you first five, sling your rifles and help yourselves to the goodies."

He thrust open the haversack and one by one, hesitantly in most cases, the five men picked out two lumps of the plastic

107

explosives and two pencils. Doan took the remaining two blocks himself and whispered. "Right, fellers, spread out. You guys for boat number four. You other two, follow me, we'll take the number three. Okay, Let's go!"

Swiftly, bodies bent double, the little group ran along the sea-wall and without hesitation dropped on to the battle-littered jetty below. Now they could see the outlines of the two sleek E-boats clearly and the dark purposeful figures of the German seamen in their gleaming leather suits and little side-hats getting them ready to move out. They split up and Doan saw to his relief that there was no sentry posted at the little gangplank which led to both boats. That was going to help, he told himself. They would have to get on the boats, plant their charges and be off within a matter of minutes and they could not afford to be stopped by anything or anybody. He ran up the swaying gangplank followed by the others. Nobody took any notice of them. The German sailors were too busy with their own tasks, and probably took the newcomers for crew members. Doan didn't wait to find out. He doubled across to the grill which covered the engine and tossed in a lump of the smelly plastic explosive, having first pulled the pin which triggered the "pencil". A couple of feet away, another man stuck a block of it to the vessel's funnel, while a seaman, who'd narrowly missed colliding with a hurrying German, simply flung his first piece down a companionway. Within seconds, all of them had got rid of their explosive charges, without having been spotted. Doan waved his hand. It was the signal to clear the boat.

Not a moment too soon. Already a German sailor, feet braced apart to take the strain, was standing at the bow, ready to cast off. The Englishmen doubled across the gangplank. Someone shouted something behind them. But they ran on. A second later, the E-boat's skipper rapped out an order over the tannoy system. The seaman on the bow threw his line to the quay. The E-boat's motors burst into full, frantic life. The night was hideous with noise. The boat shuddered, like a racing dog straining at the leash. Swiftly she started to pull away, the water churned to a bright cream at her bow, as her props began to revolve with ever increasing speed. Immediately her companion began to follow her.

Doan sprang up on to the sea wall. "All right, Petty Officer," he yelled above the roar, "let's get the hell out of here."

"At the double!" the P.O. commanded.

His ten men broke up their defensive semi-circle and started to run after Doan and the others. Nobody wanted to be last now. They all knew the balloon would go up in a couple of minutes and they wanted to be back on the whaler and out in the harbour first.

Doan almost ran into an old woman, pushing a wounded civilian on a wheel-barrow. *"Sale boche!"* she cried and taking off one of her wooden sabots, flung it after the hurrying Englishmen.

"Compliments of our French allies," Doan yelled gaily, as it narrowly missed him.

"Ruddy frogs!" the Petty Officer grunted at his side. "If you ask me —" His words ended in a sudden warning. "Look out, sir! Jerries to the front — *uhg!*" Scarlet flame stabbed the darkness with terrifying suddenness and he screamed as the first burst of German machine-gun fire ripped open the front of his chest. Rose Force had walked right into a new German road-block!

# SEVEN

"Slow ahead," Commander Lamb said softly into the voice-tube.

Below, the *Rose's* engines almost died away immediately and her speed slackened at once to a mere five knots.

"Hard-a-starboard, cox'n!" he ordered without looking round, his anxious eyes searching the entrance to the *Avant Porte* directly in front, for any sign of Rose Force's whaler.

"Hard-a-starboard, sir!" Degenhardt echoed dutifully, back at the wheel, now that he was no longer needed at the depth-charge launcher.

Lamb held up his watch at an angle so that he could see its luminous dial better. "Damn," he cursed out loud. Doan's thirty minutes were almost up and still there was no whaler hurrying out of the twin claws of concrete which made up the entrance to the port.

He leant over to the voice-pipe, as Degenhardt completed the manoeuvre behind him. "Stop starboard," he ordered. The bell clanged. Now the *Rose* was almost motionless, presenting her blunt bow to the harbour, ready to swing the whaler aboard and run for it immediately.

Lamb walked to the side of the bridge and looked back. Every man was at his battle station and he could see the lookouts on both sides of the ship, searching the stretch of sea between them and the burning town for any sign of the missing whaler. "Damn," he said again and decided to count to a hundred before he next looked at his watch. But his anxiety was too overpowering. He looked at it before he had even reached twenty. Doan had exactly five minutes left! He hammered his fist against the bulkhead and demanded of the darkness: "Where the hell are they?"

His question remained unanswered.

He walked to the centre of the bridge again. Degenhardt avoided his gaze. The old German knew what must be going through the Captain's head at this moment. Doan had been with him ever since '40. They were drinking and whoring pals — in moderation as far as the Captain was concerned, for the *Rose* was his only real love — but in five minutes, Commander Lamb would have to sacrifice Doan and all the rest of Rose Force. And Degenhardt knew he would. The ship was more important than Doan and his men. Always, inevitably, HMS *Rose* came first. If the American failed to return within the next five minutes, the Captain would abandon him to his fate.

Lamb bent over the voice-pipe again. "Chief, get ready to give me all you've got —"

"Sir," a frightened voice cut into his words. "Sir, Torpedo boats — Jerry torpedo boats!"

Lamb straightened up at once. On the top of "A" turret, a look-out was waving frantically and pointing to the exit from the harbour. He swung up his night glasses and gasped with surprise, knowing as he identified the sleek, rakish E-boats, whose prows were already beginning to rise high out of the water as their skippers gave them full power, that Doan had failed to carry out his task.

Then it happened; the first German star shell curved in a burning arc above them and X-turret opened up with a thump that shook the almost motionless destroyer. The first E-boat stopped abruptly as if it had hit an invisible wall. A great gout of brilliant white flame shot upwards and then descending again, seared along the whole length of the wooden craft.

What happened next was etched indelibly on the minds of the watchers on the *Rose*. Those of them who survived the war never forgot it. Suddenly the first boat erupted into a mass of roaring flames and her crew became insane human torches, running back and forth, thrashing at the burning leather with claws that burned, too. Some flung themselves overboard. But the water was on fire too, flooded with the burning oil. Frantically the swimmers fought to survive, striking out desperately for the seawall. They had no chance. The flames devoured them in their scarlet, greedy, all-consuming maws, ripping them open, turning their white flesh into a black bubbling pulp, until finally they were gone altogether.

But the horror was not over yet. The skipper of the other E-boat swung round his stricken mate in a wild curve of churning white water and came on in again, 20 mm flak cannon pouring a solid wall of red tracer shells at the stationary British destroyer. X-turret, slow and leisurely in comparison, took up the challenge. But when it seemed that nothing could stop the E-boat's daring run-in, with her shells punching hole after hole in the *Rose's* superstructure, there was a monstrous crash of explosive. The E-boat seemed to leap high into the air. When it came down again, it was broken into two halves, each separate half awash with burning oil, with the dead and dying crewmen lying on the deck, tracer exploding all around them in a lunatic firework display, while the searing flame burnt them to charred cinders, spines arched in agonized bows, skeletal arms flung out in piteous convulsive crucifixion.

Just at that moment the lookout on "A" Current who had first spotted the E-boats sang out in frenzied fear: "Torpedo port —"

His words ended in a scream of pain, as the E-boat's torpedo struck the *Rose* just below the forward mess-deck and flung him on to the steel deck below, as if a giant fist had propelled him. As he died, his face smashed to pulp, drowning in his blood, HMS *Rose* came slowly and inevitably to a complete stop.

# *EIGHT*

Doan's men crouched behind a wall, faces tense and grim.
The unexpected burst of German fire which had felled a quarter of
their number had unnerved them. Apart from a couple of the sailors
who risked their necks to poke their rifles around the corner and fire
off a quick shot at the German road-block barring their way back to
the whaler, they were numb and apathetic with fright.

Doan knew that they had to move — and move soon. It
wouldn't take long for the Germans to start sending out troops to
outflank them. "Chalky," he called hoarsely to Leading Seaman
White, a veteran of forty-odd and one of those who kept returning
the German fire.

"Sir?"

"You got any grenades left?"

"Two, sir."

"Good man. Prepare to throw them when I give the word."

"Ay, ay, sir."

Doan turned to the others crouched in line behind the wall.
"Now listen," he snapped, raising his voice against the renewed
chatter of the German machine gun at the roadblock, "the only
people who stay here are going to be the dead ones. If we don't
move soon, the Krauts will. So we've got to beat them to the draw.
When I give the word, we're gonna run like hell across the road and
over that wall. God knows what's behind it. We'll find out. We'll
find our way beyond the Krauts along there, and make it back to the
whaler."

"But they'll see us, sir," someone quavered — one of the new hands, Doan thought.

"Of course, they'll goddam well see us!" Doan answered. "But that's a chance we've got to take." He lifted up the muzzle of his tommy gun and tapped the sole remaining magazine to check if it was correctly in place. "All right, those who are coming with me, get to their feet. I'm about to take off." Reluctantly they rose, one by one. *All* of them. Doan smiled to himself; his pep talk had worked. "All right, Chalky, get ready with those grenades."

"Ready when you're ready, sir," The old hand answered, his voice completely steady and under control.

"NOW!"

Chalky threw his first grenade almost leisurely and they were up and running at once.

*"Die hauen ab!"* a voice cried in German.

Instantly, Chalky's grenade exploded directly on the machine gun and its frightening chatter died at once. But slugs from the German's rifles were still hitting the cobbles all around them. A rating went down just in front of Doan. He bent down and pulled the man to his feet. "Keep going ... for God's sake, keep going!" he gasped dragging the man with him.

Behind them, Chalky White came out from his cover and standing in full view of the Germans threw his last grenade, just as a slug buried itself deep inside his skinny chest, below the fading blue tattoo of "Honour or Death". It slammed him against the wall, where he died, sliding slowly down its length, his eyes glazed and turned upwards, a faint mocking smile on his thin, whitening lips.

His grenade exploded behind the barricade, flinging its German defenders about like puppets in the hands of a crazy puppeteer. And then the handful of sailors were scrambling frantically over the brick wall and running blindly through the garden beyond. They had made the break successfully.

A mile away, a very worried Commander Lamb was still considering how he was going to make his own particular break with the *Rose*. Already the first alarming reports of the damage to his beloved ship had come flashing up to the bridge. The ship had been holed underwater — no one knew how badly yet. The explosion had

114

also buckled the deck plating of the fo'c'sle and dragged it down to such an extent that "A" turret's twin 5 inchers were now pointing absurdly, straight down at the sea.

But worst of all, something had fouled the engines, for the *Rose* had lost power at once after she had been hit by the German "fish".

Anxiously Lamb waited for Degenhardt to come back from below and report, while fire and damage control parties rushed frantically across the crazily tilted desk, and the gunners — including MacFadden and Wide Boy rigging up a Lewis gun on top of the now useless "A" turret — stood by to return fire as soon as the German batteries discovered that they had a crippled British destroyer right in their own backyard.

"Come on," Lamb cried, drumming his fingers impatiently on the bridgehead, "come on, Degenhardt."

He heard the clatter of Degenhardt's old-fashioned nailed seaboots on the companion-way, and swung round. "Well?" he demanded.

"Bad, sir," the old CPO gasped.

"The engines?"

"As far as the Chief ER knows at this moment, they're okay —"

"Thank God for that," Lamb exclaimed in relief. "For God's sake, then, let's get under way."

"That's the catch, sir."

"What do you mean, Chief?"

"Don't know how it happened, sir, but it must have been a freak explosion —"

"Get on with it," Lamb interrupted impatiently.

"Sir," Degenhardt said hurriedly, "half the stokers and engine-room personnel have been killed or wounded. The place is a bloody shambles down there. They're lying all over the show."

"Oh, my God!" Lamb checked himself. At moments like this, he knew a captain must be above emotion. In a crisis he had to lead, set an example, not give way to his feelings, however powerful they might be. "What's the hold-up then?"

"They got to get the engine room tidied up, check for

damage —"

"No time for that now. Get back down there at once" (the telegraph was out), Lamb commanded with calculated brutality, "and tell the ER.9 to get the engines started at once. I'll see that the wounded and the dead are taken care of as soon as possible. Off you go, now!"

"Ay, ay, sir." He hesitated for a fraction of a second. "And Mr Doan's whaler, sir? We could use the men now if we're going to —"

Again Commander Lamb interrupted the little petty officer brutally. "I have no time for Mr Doan's party now, CPO. They'll have to take their chances like the rest of us. The *Rose* comes first. Now get on with it, man! ..."


Twice they had dodged parties of German soldiers searching for them in the confused mess of the Old Town, springing over garden walls, doubling frantically down back alleys with angry tracers stitching a deadly pattern at their heels, shouldering in locked doors and trampling through little houses to the accompaniment of screams and curses in French. Once Doan, finding a door impossible to break down, went head-first through a window and landed on the floor of somebody's kitchen, gazing up bewilderedly at the breakfast things laid out on a blue checked, frayed tablecloth. They seemed so unreal.

They found an abandoned wood-burning German truck and tried to start it in the hope that they could bull their way in it through the Germans, who now seemed to be everywhere. But all the man at the wheel, fumbling in the glowing darkness with unfamiliar controls succeeded in doing, was to turn the truck's headlights full on.

"Put out that bloody light, will yer!" a rating standing next to the winded Doan yelled angrily, just before the enemy Spandau sent an angry burst of bullets winging their way. And then they were off running again, hearts beating frantically with fear.

Now they were grouped in what looked like a paint warehouse, with rows of neatly stacked blue cans everywhere. To their right, a multiple German flak cannon was chattering away frenetically, firing flat out, tearing the little French houses to its front to pieces. Scarlet flames were beginning to rise from the ground. But it wasn't the flak cannon which was holding up what was left of Rose Force; it was the sniper ensconced in a tumble down wooden shed, immediately ahead of them, barring the way to the sea wall and the whaler. Anyone attempting to leave the cover of the paint warehouse, would hear the dry crack of the hidden German's rifle and a slug would whine off the wall frighteningly close to the seaman's head.

"Hell," Doan exclaimed, "the bastard has really got us bottled up." He crashed his clubbed fist against the wall in frustration. The whaler could only be a matter of yards away and just one single man, armed with a rifle, prevented their escape.

"Sir," a young voice broke through his frustrated anger.

"What is it?" Doan swung round and stared at the new hand crouching there, his young face greasy in the ruddy, reflected light of the burning old town.

"I found this." He thrust a can at Doan.

"Found *what?*"

"Well, it looks like petrol or turps to me, sir, and I thought we could —"

"*Gas!* Of course," Doan beat him to it, "that's the way. Okay, don't stand there like a spare penis at a wedding, man, get the cap off."

"Ay, ay, sir!" the young hand snapped back with alacrity. Hastily he unscrewed the cap. The air was suddenly heavy with the stink of petrol.

Doan smiled suddenly and raised the tommy-gun. This was going to be a real Texas-style turkey shoot, he promised himself, as the sailor poised himself behind him, can in hand. "Okay, when I yell "Move", fling the can at that wooden shed — and for Chrissake, don't miss, do you hear?"

"Ay, ay, sir."

"Okay — *move!*"

The new hand lunged past Doan and raising his arm high like a bowler, hurtled the can at the shed, just before the sniper's rifle cracked once again, his bullet narrowly missing the young sailor's head.

Doan counted five, forcing himself by sheer willpower to count slowly, giving the fumes of petrol time to rise and cover the front of the shed. Then he sprang to his feet, legs spread apart like an old-style Texas gunslinger, tommy gun tucked in hard against his right hip, and let the front of the shed have a full burst of tracer.

For one long second nothing happened. Suddenly there was a great hush like the sound of a huge primeval monster drawing breath. Next moment the whole front of the shed was burning furiously, and the German sniper was writhing frantically on the cobbles, a human torch, whose very hands, with which he was trying to beat out the flames wreathing his body, were already on fire.

"At the double!" Doan yelled triumphantly. "Follow me Rose Force!"

As they passed the man dying in agony, someone emptied a magazine into him. His violent writhing stopped and as they ran on towards the sea wall, he lay there still, the blue flames eating away his head — almost leisurely ...


The engine room was hectic with comings and goings. The dead had been bundled unceremoniously into a corner and covered by a greasy, oil-stained tarpaulin. Now the sick berth attendants were beginning to move out the wounded and make room for the men still alive and uninjured to begin the necessary emergency repairs. A telegraphist, his naked back one huge livid purple bruise, was working on the main switchboard, pulling through a length of thick insulated cable and connecting it up. A stoker was hammering at one of the main steam valves with a wooden mallet, while his mate, inexplicably completely naked and revealing the full glory of the tattooed mouse disappearing into his anus, was wrenching away at a section of piping further on, with a huge spanner, half as big as himself.

Lamb took it all in at a glance, and saw that the grizzled Scots Chief had the situation well in hand.

"Well?" he demanded.

The Chief wiped the beads of sweat from his brow. "Ay, she'll move all right. But yon port engine'll give us trouble. I'm afeared that bluidy Jerry fish knocked the shaft out."

Lamb absorbed the information quickly. "It's all right, Chief, as long as we've one screw. With that mess up top and the water coming in the way it is, we're not going to be able to make more than a few knots anyway."

"Ay, no doubt yell be right, there, sir," the Scots engineer replied, his red strained eyes following the activities of his staff all the time as he spoke to the captain.

Lamb hesitated only for an instant before he asked the overwhelming question: "When do you think you'll be able to steam, Chief?"

The craggy-faced, ER.9 flashed a quick look at the man working on the telegraph and the two stokers at the main steam valve. "Five minutes, sir — ten at the most."

Lamb's face lit up suddenly. "Excellent, Chief, really a fine job of work!"

"Thank ye, sir. And how far is it to go, if I may ask, sir?" he queried, eyes still everywhere.

"Nearly three hundred, I'd guess."

The Chief whistled. *"Three hundred!"*

Lamb broke away, but at the foot of the ladder, he paused and called over his shoulder, "Don't you worry, Chief. Just you keep the elastic tight which makes the *Rose* move, and I'll get you home to that nice little up-homers you've got going in Pompey."

The engine-room staff laughed at the sally, while the Chief flushed crimson at the mention of his relationship with the buxom widow, who wasn't his wife — the wife was safely tucked away in Glasgow! Then Lamb was climbing the rungs of the ladder two at a time.

"What's it like, sir?" Degenhardt asked anxiously when he returned to the bridge.

"Better than I thought. We'll make steam in ten minutes at the outside."

"Thank God for that, sir," Degenhardt breathed fervently.

119

"Yes, you can say that again, CPO. Our luck's not going to hold out much longer. They must spot us soon."

"What about the trim, sir?" Degenhardt asked, indicating the crumpled bow. "By now she must be drawing six or seven feet more than her normal sixteen."

"I know that, but it can't be helped. The main thing is that we get underway at once. As soon as we're off this damned coast, we'll start tossing as much stuff overboard as possible and see if we can't correct the trim that way."

"What kind of speed do you think we're going to make, sir? Degenhardt asked, persisting in his questions while the Captain had time. It also took his mind off that terrible possibility, that at any moment the Germans might discover the presence of the stricken *Rose* right beneath their gun barrels!

Lamb sighed. "Not much more than five knots for a start, Degenhardt."

"It'll take a devil of a long time for us to get to England, sir."

"Maybe. But we must hope that we can restore trim. Then we can —"

"Signal flare, sir!" Scouse MacFadden roared from his post next to the Lewis Gun on "A" turret. "To port, sir."

Lamb turned swinging up his night glasses. Two green flares were slowly descending towards the water, colouring it an unnatural, sickly hue. To the east, white and red tracer started to zip flatly across the entrance to the harbour, gathering speed rapidly, as it got ever closer to the place from which the flares had come. "It's the signal, Degenhardt," Lamb said excitedly. "It's Mr Doan and Rose Force!"

"Thank God for that, sir," Degenhardt exclaimed, and CPO Horst Degenhardt was not exactly a pious man. "Thank God for that ..."


Five minutes later, Doan, his helmet and most of his eyebrows gone from the exploding petrol, his face black and begrimed, reported to the bridge. "And I thought we made it," he exclaimed morosely, sweeping his hand out at the ruined fo'c'sle.

"You made it all right, Number One," Lamb said encouragingly. "Unfortunately, one of the bastards managed to get off a fish before he blew up. You can see the result."

"That I can, skipper." Grimly Doan wiped the scum off his lips giving him an odd resemblance to a black minstrel. "And now?"

"And now?" Lamb echoed his question, thinking back on the places the *Rose* had taken them and the action they had seen together, as if the ship were a live thing and not a man-made product of the Jarrow shipyards. Suddenly he was overcome by a completely foolish and emotional idea: the *Rose* had done so much for them; they could not just abandon her like that. "And now?" he repeated, as the first delightful shiver of the deck beneath his feet indicated that the ER.9 had got the engines, or at least, one of them, started again. "Why now, Number One, we're going to sail her across the Channel — to England, Home and Beauty."

"Ay, ay, sir," Doan answered dutifully as he told himself it was going to be one bitch of a long haul. But he kept that particular thought to himself.

# The Long Voyage Home

# ONE

There were perhaps forty, immaculately uniformed, posturing *Kriegsmarine* and *Wehrmacht* officers, of the kind the ordinary sailor and soldier called "the base stallions" on the steeply sloping, battle-littered deck of HMS *Campbelltown* when it happened. On the dock there could have been another four hundred German troops, staring at the destroyer's crazily crumpled bow and passing the time pleasantly enough in idle conjecture on British reasons for going to so much trouble to ram the dock gate with such an old tub. Behind them, the last of the Tommy prisoners were being taken out of the bar of the cafe *La Boule* to the waiting trucks. It was noon on March 28th, 1942. Soon all of them, apart from the prisoners who naturally didn't deserve it, would be returning to their various barracks, ships, and messes on this grey wartime Saturday to eat the traditional fare of that day — thick green pea soup with sausage, with weak French beer to wash it down if they were "other rankers" and good strong, red wine from the South if they were gentlemen and officers (the French of the Unoccupied Zone were an eminently practical people; they didn't disdain the German *Reichsmark).*

So they looked and talked and gestured, while their stomachs rumbled, for in the German Armed Forces, breakfast consisted only of weak *ersatz* coffee and bread. Their thoughts were of the afternoon or evening they would spend in one of the port's many brothels. Or if they were officers, of their French mistresses — all frizzed, black-dyed hair, platform heels made of wood, thin knee-length floral dresses — making *l'amour à la française,* and everybody knew what wonderful degenerate piggery the French women made — no decent German woman would do things "like that".

Then it happened!

There was a thick low roar, which grew in fury by the instant, overwhelming everything else — all thoughts of thick green pea soup, weak French beer, good red wine, the wonderful degenerate piggery — smashing forth from the wildly bucking deck beneath their feet, spilling scarlet flame, filling the air with its thick yellow, choking cordite fumes, hurling them high into the grey noon air, tossing and turning their bodies in wild confusion, like paper playthings of the wind.

HMS *Campbelltown's* five tons of high explosive had been detonated dead on time! As the French and German military ambulances and fire-engines raced to the scene of death and destruction, the narrow frightened streets frenzied with their noise and the thin howl of their sirens, those of the spectators who had survived the great explosion realized in their agonies *why* the British had rammed the dock gate of the *Forme Ecluse.*

The German troops throughout the port lost control of themselves, as more and more delayed charges began to explode everywhere. They fired indiscriminately at the French workers returning home for their midday meal, satchels under their arms, the usual cheap cigarette glued to their lower lips. The French panicked. They broke across the one surviving bridge crossing the *Forme Ecluse* to the *Bassin Penhouet.* The German fire intensified as the panic-stricken workers spread out across the dock area, leaving their dead and dying sprawled out on the bloody *pavé.* A troop of khaki-clad German workers of the *Organization Todt\** tried to stop the French, who simply swept through the unarmed German workers. Next, the soldiers thinking the Todt men were commandos poured a frantic ruthless hail of fire into them. They went down by the score.

Jean Marchais, tucked away in his hiding place right at the top of the old 18th century house, frowned and then chuckled as the white-haired senile landlady poured the unlovely contents of her chamber-pot on the heads of the Boche soldiers advancing after the

* German Labour Force

fleeing workers below and then, as an afterthought, dropped the chamber-pot itself upon them. Then his grin vanished and judging this moment of absolute confusion as good as any to avoid the German radio detection vans, (which had suddenly appeared everywhere this morning after the raid) he thrust on his earphones and began working his transmitter key with a swift, expert forefinger and thumb.

London received the message and deciphered it one hour later. At two, it was in Mountbatten's hands. Thirty minutes later his staff car was hurrying through London on its way to 10 Downing Street, trying to catch the Prime Minister before he disappeared for the week-end to his secret retreat in the country.

Churchill saw Mountbatten at once. "You don't need to tell me, Mountbatten," he cried, cigar in hand, face flushed from a very good lunch. "It worked!"

"Like a charm, sir. Tenth Anti-Submarine Striking Force broke WIT silence an hour ago. Now we've just received a message from the SOE* man in the port that the *Campbelltown* — which rammed the lock-gate well and truly — has just exploded. All five tons of explosive went up at noon." He beamed across at the Prime Minister.

Churchill dropped his cigar on to the oak writing table and clasped his pudgy, nicotine-stained hands together, as if in prayer. "Thank God, Mountbatten! That puts paid to the *Tirpitz's* venture into the great ocean." He dabbed his wet eyes and tried to restrain his emotions, which pleased Mountbatten, the aristocrat to his fingertips, who hated to see the Prime Minister cry. It wasn't the first time he had done so, nor would it be the last. Crying, he always thought, was so very plebeian. "And the casualties, Mountbatten?" he asked, the fruity, port-heavy voice suddenly very thin and fearful.

"The Second Commando bought it rather heavily," Mountbatten answered carefully.

"How heavily?"

* SOE was a branch of wartime intelligence.

"Most of the ORs and nearly all the officers didn't come back."

"Oh, this damned war —" Churchill squeezed back the tears. "The Navy, Mountbatten?" he asked in a tight, thin voice. "What do you know of the Navy's losses?"

"Most of the motor launches have bought it. According to Commander Ryder on the *Tynedale,* there might be — at the most — six of them making their way back, some of them independently."

"And the destroyers themselves?"

"Both the *Atherstone* and the *Tynedale* are well on their way home now, sir. They are due for air cover from Coastal Command at sixteen hundred hours today."

"Excellent, Mountbatten." Churchill beamed up at him.

"There is the *Rose* though, sir."

"The *Rose?*"

"Yessir, commanded by Lt-Commander Lamb. She has been missing since before dawn. She must have carried out her mission, however, because the German torpedo boats did not attack the rest of the Force."

"Do you think she has been lost, Mountbatten?"

"I don't know, sir. Our agent over there has not mentioned any such loss and he is regarded in Baker Street* as highly reliable."

Churchill thought for a moment, then said, "Mountbatten, please ensure that all — and I mean, *all* — attempts are made to give her assistance if she is still afloat and needs it."

"Naturally, sir," Mountbatten answered promptly, wondering as he spoke if the Prime Minister really knew just how difficult his request would be to fulfill. HMS *Rose,* or so it seemed, had completely vanished off the face of the seas. If she were still unsunk, she could be anywhere ...

* HQ of the SOE organization

# TWO

At that particular moment, Lt-Commander John Lamb was shaving in half a mug of soapy Newcastle Brown Ale. The explosion had knocked out both fresh and salt water pumps. Now the crew of the *Rose* had been put on ration of two bottles a beer per day from the ship's store — for all purposes. Thus he scraped industriously at his face, pausing to have a sip of the beer remaining in the bottle and a bite of the great, thick corned-beef sandwich — the galley fires had blown out — which was the first food he had eaten since the previous day. Beneath him the *Rose* plodded on doggedly towards England at an impossibly slow five knots.

Satisfied with his appearance, Lamb dried his face, ate the last of the wad and slipped into his duffle coat, ready to go outside. A thick, freezing cold fog engulfed the ship, which was exceedingly fortunate for them under their present circumstances; it would certainly give them the cover they needed when they began what they must do, if they were ever to get back to port.

On the quarter deck, a leading hand was sewing yet another canvas around one of the bodies which lay in neat rows to both sides of him, concluding the grisly business by thrusting his curved sailmaker's needle through the dead man's pinched, white nose to satisfy himself that he was really dead. "The last stitch", the old hands called this survival from the days of Nelson and his wooden men-o'-war. Lamb shuddered and asked hastily, "how many?"

The man looked up from his task and replied at once, knowing exactly what the captain wanted to know. "Forty, sir, two officers and thirty-eight ratings — and happen there'll be a couple

129

more down in yon fo'c'sle. T'were a quick death, though, sir," he added in his mournful West Riding accent. "They must have snuffed it reet away."

"Yes, I suppose so. Thank you."

As Lamb walked away and the leading hand began stitching up yet another body, he did a quick calculation. With Doan's losses and the wounded down in the sick bay, the *Rose* must have lost sixty men, about a quarter of the crew, including the two officers, both new subs who had only just joined her. He shook his head in dismay. He would have a lot of letters to write to the next-of-kin, once they got back to port (and he didn't doubt they would). But then in these last two terrible years on the *Rose* he had had plenty of experience in writing those sad, compassionate letters to the relatives of those who had died on her.

Doan and Degenhardt were waiting for him on the fo'c'sle. Doan looked his usual cheery self. Like Lamb he had taken a couple of hours' catnap, once the *Rose* had succeeded in vanishing into the dawn fog off the French coast.

"You're looking very sprightly, Number One," he commented.

"It's my new after-shave, sir. Eau de Newcastle Ale."

Lamb chuckled. "I know it well. But I bet it's not particularly popular with the lower deck. I'm sure they'd rather drink it than shave in it."

"They're all shaven, sir," Degenhardt said ominously. "Or they'd better be! If I catch one of them filthy dirty, they'll be straight on the rattle."

"I'm sure they will, CPO — I'm sure," Lamb appeased him. "Now then, let's have a look-see at the damage."

Together they walked cautiously to the edge of the wrecked section of the foredeck. Before them the twenty-odd foot of deck was twisted and contorted grotesquely, with the bullring on the *Rose's* buckled bow hardly more than three feet out of the water. Raise the destroyer's speed to her full thirty knots and she would go under, Lamb knew that.

Ignoring the unpleasant hollow thud-thud from below, which could indicate that a heavy piece of equipment had been shaken

130

loose by the explosion and was smashing itself against the already damaged bulkhead whenever the ship hit a wave, Lamb took hold of the rail and looked over the side.

A thick bluish oil was leaking from somewhere, unpleasantly. It looked, Lamb thought with disgust, like pus seeping from a badly septic wound. But of the wound itself — the great hole the torpedo must have caused — he could see nothing. It was below the water-line; and in a way he was both worried — because he could not ascertain the degree of damage — and glad — because he hated to see the *Rose* hurt. She had been hurt enough over the years.

"Doesn't look too rosy, eh, skipper?" Doan ventured.

"No, it's not exactly a pleasing prospect on a grey foggy day like this in the middle of nowhere," he answered slowly and turned to Degenhardt. "What of the W/T*, CPO?"

"Still out sir and looking as if it's gonna be for a long time to come. Sparks says the main switchboard has blown for a start."

Lamb nodded his understanding. "All right, that means we can't expect any help from anyone but ourselves — at least for the time being until Sparks gets his set repaired."

"In a way, it's good, sir," Doan said thoughtfully, "Jerry might get a fix on us like that ..." His words trailed away as he realized that the Captain was not really listening; his gaze was fixed intently on the mess of the fo'c'sle, as if he were coming to a decision.

"Right! This is the way we're going to do it. Come on both of you."

A minute later he was on the bridge, loud-hailer in his hand. Through force of habit he blew through it, to check it. The metallic roar of his breath, magnified many times over by the speakers pointing forward and aft, alerted the crew working on the deck and they turned to the bridge. Lamb looked at their faces. They were shaved, as Degenhardt had ordered, but most of them were grey and dull, as if they were astonished that the old *Rose* had lasted so long and unable to believe she could survive much longer.

"Attention, please. This is the Captain speaking." Lamb's

* Wireless-telegraphy, i.e. radio room

131

voice overcame the howl of the wind, which made the crew's gear flap around their bodies. "I want to tell you what we are now going to do, so that you're all in the picture."

There was no reaction to his mild attempt at humour, and they continued to stare up at him mutely. Instinctively Lamb knew he must put some fire into them, make them believe that they were going to be able to do it, for he would need the utmost from every man of them if he were going to get *Rose* back to England. And he was absolutely determined that he would.

"Now as you all know, we've been pretty badly hit and some very good chaps have been killed. All the same, the situation — if serious — is not desperate. Please understand that. We can make it, if everyone of you chaps pulls his weight."

Standing just behind Lamb, listening to his words, Doan could not help thinking that he sounded awfully like one of those upper-class English actors in those terribly "British" movies they made before the war. Leslie Banks in *Sanders of the River* or Ronald Colman in one of the epics of the Empire. Yet he knew too, that this was the way to treat the British sailor, who had none of the disbelieving, easy cynicism of the average American lower deck gob, with his inevitable chewing-gum. The English could still be inspired.

"I've got three measures in mind," Lamb was saying, "which I think should put us in a much better position. That is, if we can pull them off quickly, while we're still covered from Jerry air attack by this fog. One, we must get more buoyancy by pumping out as much water as possible from the fo'c'sle. I know the suction line is gone, but we can do it by hand. Then we might be able to plug the hole the torpedo caused or failing that to seal off part of the compartment."

"That's a ruddy lot of mights, Scouse," Wide Boy, standing next to the Liverpudlian grunted.

But Scouse ignored him. A new hope was beginning to dawn on his drawn face — and he was not alone in his hope.

"Two," Lamb went on. "We'll get rid of all surplus weight. The barrels of the 5-inchers in "A" turret will go for a start. We can't fire them anyway." The Captain smiled at MacFadden. "Sorry,

132

Scouse. But we'll provide you with some new peashooters, once we're back."

This time his mention of MacFadden's nickname and the mild joke worked. There was a ripple of laughter and MacFadden even blushed at the attention he had received from the Captain.

"It doesn't matter, sir," he said automatically, knowing that the Captain couldn't hear him at that distance, but wanting to say it all the same.

"Three." Lamb ticked off the measures, by raising his free hand so that they could see. "We must try to get rid of the anchor cable and the anchors. They weigh a devil of a lot and once we get them out, I hope our trim will improve considerately. Now I know we've got to manhandle the damn things out and that's going to be a back-breaking job. But there is no other way. The cable's got to go!"

Lamb paused momentarily. "I shall read the burial service for the dead in about thirty minutes. I'd like all hands to attend and then we get started. And I don't need to mention how vital it is that every man does his bit, if we're going to get back." His voice rose. "And we *will* get back, you know." Someone in the crowd shouted hoarsely and emotionally. "Three cheers for the skipper and the old *Rose, lads!* ... Come on now, hip-hip!"

As the cheers began to ring out, Lamb's mouth dropped open in sheer, undisguised amazement. The men were actually cheering him for making them risk their necks even more, when secretly every one of them must be thinking how much easier it would be to give up and surrender to the Germans. Overcome, he blundered off the bridge to get things started.

# THREE

They worked their guts out all that long grey afternoon, while the look-outs — and Lamb could only afford two of them, port and starboard, searched the low cloud anxiously and unceasingly for the first winged shapes which would mean the end of HMS *Rose*.

Without difficulty, the hand derrick had been used to lift out the 5-inchers' useless barrels and Scouse, almost happily (although he had looked after them like an old hen with her chicks ever since they had been first installed in 1940), supervised their depositing into the sea.

The dumping of the anchor chain and the anchors had presented more difficulty. As there was no power available to drag the chain up, they had been forced to use the ratchet-and-pawl lever to get it out, link by link with four men, their faces greasy with sweat and strain, operating the lever, their muscles threatening to burst at every fresh murderous stroke.

The real trouble had started, once they had begun to attempt to pump the water out of the holed fo'c'sle. As no suction-line had been available, they had broken through the buckled deck by means of a cover-plate and begun pumping by hand. But after an hour there was no appreciable difference in the *Rose's* new trim; and Lamb knew why. "Blast it," he cried to Doan, "the bloody hole down there is too damn big! As soon as they pump it out, more water comes flooding in."

Doan wiped his forearm against his sweat-dripping brow, for he had just taken his turn with the gasping hands at the pump. "I'm afraid you're right, sir," he choked.

Lamb considered for a moment, then he made a decision.

"We're not going to get any kind of trim, Number One, with that hole still letting in enough ruddy water for a swimming pool down there," he announced. "We've got to put a patch on her."

Doan looked at him, as if he had suddenly gone crazy. "In this weather and under these conditions, sir!" he exploded, his face taut with disbelief.

"In this weather and under these conditions, Number One."

"But the water's below zero, sir."

"I know. But I'm going to ask for volunteers from the chaps dismantling the guns. They're about finished there now. We've got to get that hole plugged, if I have to go down there myself to plug it."

*"Volunteers?"* Stevens whispered to Scouse out of the side of his mouth after the Captain had finished speaking, "ferk that fer a lark! You don't get Mrs Stevens" boy doing —"

"I'll thump you good and proper, Wide Boy," MacFadden hissed threateningly," if you don't shut yer sodding cake hole." Next moment he had raised his voice and said. "Me and young Stevens here'll go, sir."

"Good show," Lamb beamed at them.

That started the ball rolling. Scouse MacFadden was a much admired man on the lower deck and a natural leader. Automatically the others followed where he went — it always seemed to pay off. And it did this time too, as the Captain explained.

"You'll go down for ten minute spells. At the end of it, CPO Degenhardt will see that you get a set of dry duds — and a tot of rum — neaters," he added, using the sailors' term for neat rum.

"Nelson's blood every ten minutes," Scouse exclaimed to the others, enthusiastically. "And that old battle-axe of a CPO acting as a chief butler and bottle-washer."

Degenhardt glowered menacingly at him, but Scouse ignored the look. "Now that's what I call a fair offer, don't you, lads!"

* * *

Thus the terrible task of patching the bulkhead began. It consisted of building a wall of planks across the gaping hole, fixed at each end by "walking sticks", or iron rods, which would eventually be caulked by the "pudding", a roll of packing-filled canvas. The water which came up to their waists deadened all feeling in the lower limbs within seconds so that at the end of their ten minute spell, the men had to be hauled out by ropes. Lying prostrate on the deck, their faces white with cold, fiery rum was forced through their lips, while other men worked their frozen limbs back and forth until the prostrate figures started to writhe with the almost unbearable agony of returning circulation.

But they went back time and time again to face that terrible burning cold. So the grey long afternoon progressed. While back in England, men returned from football matches, women curled their hair in readiness for their Saturday evening out at the pubs, and youngsters clamoured for their sweet coupons and the "flicks", the men of the *Rose* slowly completed their soul-destroying task. The wooden patch grew steadily larger. Up above, the hand pump now started to take effect. The level of the water began to fall. Thigh — knee — ankle. Finally it was just a series of greasy puddles on the metal deck and an utterly weary, blue-lipped Wide Boy was gasping like a broken old man to Scouse, "You and yer sodding volunteering, you daft scouse git!" Scouse MacFadden managed to raise a grin — but only just.


Slowly but unmistakeably the *Rose's* crumpled bow began to rise from the water. On the bridge, his second corned-beef sandwich of the day forgotten, Lamb watched the bow come up as if his life depended upon it. Doan watched him with amusement and no little compassion. The *Rose* was Lamb's whole life. This was a moment of great personal triumph for him. The *Rose* might be jinxed in the eyes of the rest of the Fleet, but she wasn't sunk yet; she was still alive and kicking.

All the same he knew time was running out. The fog was finally beginning to disperse and the silver ball of the new moon was already in the sky to the east. In its clear, cold light they would make a perfect target for any lurking Kraut U-boat — they didn't call this part of the Channel "E-Boat Alley" for nothing. "Can we afford two small cheers, skipper?" he inquired softly, purposefully malicious.

"No, three damn great big ones!" Lamb swung round on him, his bloodshot eyes shining. "All right, all right, Number One, let me have my little moment of glory. For your part, you can start working out how we're going to get to port — which port, might be better — with the master gyro compass out, and at an estimated speed of — say — ten or twelve knots."

"Ay, ay, sir!" he replied with alacrity and at once prayed that the explosion had not put the remaining magnetic compasses off.

Now all was controlled activity.

Lamb worked the bridge telegraph and picked up the voice pipe. "All right down there, Chief?" he queried, while behind him on the bridge the ratings took up their positions, under Degenhardt's eagle, if somewhat bullshot eye (he had taken his turn in the water making the patch too).

"Ready to go, sir."

"Good. All right, we'll do it nice and gently for a start. Make it thirty revs, say. No more."

"Ay, ay, sir."

"When I'm ready, I'll ring 'slow ahead'. The rest we can do by voice pipe. Then we'll try to bring her up to ten knots. Clear?"

"Clear, sir."

Lamb swung round to Doan crouched over the chart table, his eye moving back and forth from the charts to the faint green glow of the compass. "Well, Number One?" he demanded with more briskness that he felt. "What's it going to be?"

"Well, sir, assuming we're in the Channel again by now," he hesitated a moment and Lamb clapped a hand to his head in mock dismay, as if he were being spared nothing, "well assuming that, I reckon due north to Falmouth."

"Are you sure now?"

Doan grinned suddenly. "Certain, sir."

"All right," Lamb sang out to the man at the wheel, "bring her round to due north."

He rang the telegraph. There was a slight tremor. Lamb's gaze shot to the bow. Slowly the *Rose* started to move again. A faint creamy ripple appeared at both sides of her bow.

Lamb bent over the voice pipe. "Slow ahead, Chief."

The *Rose* began to pick up speed. Five knots. The creamy wash was higher now. Seven knots. Even on the bridge he could hear the metallic, hollow thud-thud of whatever was loose far down below, banging away again at the side of the bulkhead. He said a swift prayer that the damned thing wouldn't affect the patch. Behind him he felt the almost tangible tension of the others as the speed rose even higher. Ten knots!

Lamb bit his lip, thankful that the others could not see *his* tension, and craned his neck forward. The water at the *Rose's* bow was now being churned into a thick, frothy white. But the patch was holding and her trim had not changed. It was working! He felt a warm glow of triumph. HMS *Rose* was going home to England!

# FOUR

"How long you been in the Royal, Scouse?" Wide Boy asked idly, as they squatted next to their Lewis Gun, heads buried in their blue duffle coats. On the grey horizon, lay the yellow ball of the sun, as if it were too feeble to rise any further; and it was still very cold.

Scouse took the *Woodbine* out of his mouth and spat expertly over the side. "Since Nelson were a snotty," he answered.

"Come off it, Scouse. I mean it, really. How long?"

"Since '38."

Wide Boy stared at him incredulously. "You mean yer volunteered?"

"I do," Scouse answered calmly and took another *Woodbine,* from behind his right ear, lighting it with the glowing stub of the first one. "I were on the Dole. Better than the sodding workhouse. Cos that's where I would have ended, mate — in the spike."

"Cor, but to volunteer, Scouse that's going it some!" Wide Boy said.

"It all depends on the way yer look at it — as the actress said to the bishop." He cast a precautionary glance at the horizon, from whence the Jerry planes would come, if they came. It was empty. It seemed as if the grey little ghost of a crippled destroyer, plodding on at ten knots, had been abandoned by the world. She was completely alone.

"Yer know yer ought to have yer head examined, Scouse, signing on like that. When this lot is over, you'll still be in and you'll miss the pickings."

"What pickings?" Scouse looked at him curiously.

"The loot, the mazuma, the lolly, mate, that's what I mean," Wide Boy answered. "Look at my old Dad, fer instance. He won a medal in '18 and lost half his right arm winning it. But it didn't matter to him. He was all for King and Country. And what good did it do him? A ten bob a week pension and not a hope in hell of getting a job after he was demobbed. Now that's not gonna happen to yours truly. I want to be in there, right from the start, even now, getting me pinkies on some of that loot." He sneered suddenly. "It's only mugs what get caught by all this patriotism stuff."

"Oh, I don't know," Scouse said with surprising mildness for him. "There's a bunch of good lads on this ship and the officers ain't too bad either." He spat over the side again, his tough slum face suddenly very thoughtful. "Yer know, Wide Boy, I reckon that this ship is the best home I've ever had since the old lady snuffed it. It's my kind of patriotism and I think it's worth fighting for."

"Yer, yer, yer right there, Scouse," Wide Boy said excitedly, "I'm not denying that, mate. I didn't like the idea of coming on the *Rose* at first, I don't mind telling yer that. Now I know she's a shit-hot little ship. But what I'm saying is — what happens after the war is over? What then?" he thrust his sharp, handsome face close to Scouse. "Where do silly buggers like you go, when they don't need you no more. I'm asking you that!"

Scouse took his time. He knew Wide Boy was right in a way. After the war it would all fall apart, as it had done after the first lot. The officers and gents, who were so close now, would probably go their way and the ORs theirs. But perhaps they wouldn't. Perhaps they'd get something going this time which wouldn't end up in the balls-up they'd made after the first lot. Perhaps the thing they had going on the old *Rose* would continue in peacetime, spread all over the country, change things, make England a better place to live in. "Well, you see, the way I figure it Wide Boy ..."

But Scouse MacFadden never did manage to explain his own post-war philosophy to an eager Wide Boy, for at that very moment, his best oppo "Bunts", Leading Signaller Smith came bounding across the deck, crying, "Hey, Scouse, Sparks has done it!"

"Done what — pissed hissen?" Scouse cried back, his usual irreverent self once more.

"Ner," Bunts said, in no way offended. "He's gorn and got the W/T to work again. Now we can whistle up the brylcreem boys and their aeroplanes."

"Lot of ruddy pansies," Scouse said contemptuously. But there was a grin on his face all the same. If Sparks could contact home, it would not be long before the Coastal Command Sunderlands would be out in force, giving the battered old *Rose* the cover she needed so urgently.

Lamb considered Sparks' information thoughtfully, while the radio operator stared back at him, his youthful, exhausted face, flushed with triumph at the knowledge that his all-night task had finally ended in success.

"You say the dynamo is still not very good, eh, Sparks?" he asked in the end.

"Yessir. It's definitely on the blink. But I think I could do it. The signal wouldn't be very strong, but it'd reach the UK."

"I see." Lamb thought again. According to Doan's calculations they still had over one hundred and fifty sea miles to cover, and at their present speed they would not reach an English harbour till well into the next day. That would mean another day and a half of daylight when the Germans could spot them at any moment. They needed air cover from Home urgently. But there was a catch, He himself dumped the ship's secret papers and code books over the side in the first confusion after the torpedo had struck them, knowing it was vitally important that they should not fall into enemy hands. Now he would have to send details of the *Rose's* position in clear or, at the best, in some form of elementary code, vaguely remembered from his days at Dartmouth. It wouldn't take the German experts long to crack this, if they managed to pick up the message at their big radio receiving complex between Kiel and Hamburg.

"Do you think the Jerries could pick it up too?" he asked, breaking the tense silence, in which those on the bridge waited for his decision.

Sparks shrugged: "I wouldn't really know, sir. As I said, that dynamo's not too good. Its output is pretty low. Just about enough to reach England. And we have got pretty low cloud which will keep our range down. But yer never know with radio waves. Yer get freak conditions and they're picking you up in China or —"

"Thank you, Sparks," Lamb interrupted him firmly, his mind made up, "Give me fifteen minutes to dream up some sort of code and then we'll have a go. But make it quick when you're sending, very goddam quick!"

"Ay, ay, sir," the young radio operator answered eagerly. "My hand'll be moving like the proverbial fiddler's elbow."

"Just carry out orders, Sparks" replied Lamb, knowing what the man meant, and grinning in spite of himself.


*Leutnant zur See, Dr Phil. Dr Res. Nat* Helmut Quick, M.A. (Oxon) was handed the message by the head of the *B-Dienst\**, almost as soon as it was received in the *Kriegsmarine's* decoding section. "Urgent," *Korvettenkapitan* Schmidt grunted. "We think it might have something to do with that nasty business in St Nazaire. The high-ups are squawking for details. The Führer is furious, and the honour of the German Navy is at stake."

*"Geld verloren, nichts verloren. Ehre verloren, alles verloren,"\*\** the bespectacled former *Institutsdirektor und Ord. Professor der Anglistik* quoted the old German proverb at his superior, without enthusiasm.

*Kapitan* Schmidt uttered an obscenity and said without rancour, "You and your shitty proverbs! Get on with it or they'll have my shitty head up there, soon." He went out.

Professor Quick went through his usual routine with such things. First he put the *Juno Eckstein* cigarette in the little brown holder — he had always preferred the workingman's cigarette since his student days at Hamburg University; then he poured himself half a glass full of *Doppelkorn* and sniffed the contents in joyful appreciation; the pencils followed — a good half-dozen of them (he

\* The German Navy's decoding service.
\*\* Money lost, nothing lost. Honour lost, everything lost.

usually spent the long boring mornings in the office sharpening them with the same, all-consuming diligence he had once applied when polishing up his celebrated inaugural lecture on the use of the "apostrophe in Shakespeare's plays"). Finally he put both his well-polished shoes on the desk in front of him — his one concession these days, to the years he had spent at Oxford — and looked at the intercept.

He decided at once, it was the work of an amateur. The *Kriegsmarine B-Dienst* had cracked the British naval code early on in the war, but had adjusted to the fact that Admiralty, worried that the U-boats always seemed to be waiting for their supposedly top-secret Atlantic convoys, were periodically adding new variations. But this was not an attempt on the part of the "chaps" (in his own mind he always called the British 'the chaps!" because in his days at Oxford they had used that word so often) to make the old code more foolproof. This was something completely different.

He tried the old pre-war Playfair Code.

The essence of the amateur code was a key word or words. He looked at the list of letters and numbers in front of him. They were obviously divided into groups of four. Did that mean the key word had four letters? He took a drink of gin and thought about it for a bit. Outside there was no sound, save the steady pacing of the naval sentry's nail-shot jackboots on the gravel.

"But what kind of word would they use?" he asked himself after a while in English. He thought in that language when he was engaged in deciphering British intercepts; it helped.

He recalled that both the destroyers used in the St Nazaire operation had been of the Hunt Class, according to the statements of the Coastal Artillery. He tried "Hunt" as his key word and ended with a lot of gibberish.

For some time, he allowed his mind to run off in a crazy sequence of mental associations. "Hunt ... bunt ... flag ... drag ... *cunt* ... "Far too Freudian," he said aloud and stopped.

He tried another tack, playing around with an attempt to find the most frequent letter in the message, which would be the letter "e" in English in clear, as it would be in German too. It didn't work.

"Hope the buggers are not using something exotic like Welsh or Gaelic," he told himself, his glass of *Doppelkorn* half gone now. He knew it wouldn't be the first time the British had used such devices in codes and the *B-Dienst's* expert on Celtic languages was on leave at the moment, finishing his thesis for his *Habilitation,* though where the devil he expected to get a chair in the subject was beyond Quick.

He sniffed, finished the *Doppelkorn* and with unusual recklessness for him, filled up the glass again. It wasn't the best, but it was better than nothing on a long boring Sunday like this. "A rose by any other name would smell —" He stopped the quote abruptly and reaching across the desk, picked up the usual confidential handout they always received on the enemy's naval activities. Swiftly he flipped back the pages until he had the details of the St Nazaire raid. "Hunt class destroyers *Tynedale* and *Atherstone ...*" Quickly his shrewd eyes ran through the condensed account of the prisoners' statements . "MTB ... *Motor Gunboat (MGB) 314...* HMS *Campbelltown.*"

And then he had it. "A dying sailor found on the seawall of the *Avant Porte* stated, after persistent questioning (and Quick knew what Naval Intelligence meant by "persistent questioning"; obviously the Gestapo had been at work at St Nazaire) that he was a member of the crew of an English destroyer HMS *Rose ..*

"Bingo!" Quick clicked his fingers together excitedly in his English working class imitation. "The *Rose* — his four letter word!"

"Rosemarie, my darling," he sang gaily, in his imitation of Nelson Eddy in his uniformed prime, as a very unlikely Canadian Mountie, while he scribbled away furiously, using the new key word.

Immediately the letters and the numbers began to fit into place. Transposing vertically, and then horizontally when the first attempt failed to make sense, his excitement rising all the time, he saw the message begin to emerge on the yellow block in front of him. "HMS *Rose ... torpedoed off St Nazaire ... making way home ... believed position ... latitude ...*"

He pressed the bell on his desk. Instead of the naval orderly, Schmidt himself appeared. "Got a new job?" Quick queried, pleased with himself.

"I probably will have soon, if you don't get that message cracked", Schmidt grunted. "Top deck is decidedly wet and windy at this particular moment. They say Raeder himself* has been summoned to the Führer HQ to explain how the British got away with it at St Nazaire. The chips are flying exceedingly thick and fast — as *you* would say."

"As I would say," Quick said in English which Schmidt spoke as well as he did himself, and handing him the deciphered intercept, "April is the cruellest month. And tomorrow is April the first, if my memory serves me rightly."

Schmidt's eyes flashed through it. *"Touché!"* he snapped with sudden excitement. "It looks as if we have got one of the naughty Navy, doesn't it," he said, speaking English too.

"Rather," Helmut Quick drawled in a fair imitation of the grand young men he had so admired in the halcyon days of 1930. As Schmidt went out hurriedly, precious message in hand, he wondered idly whether he should not perhaps begin to associate himself more with the group around Professor Gundolf in Munich, who subscribed to the theory that Shakespeare was really German. After all, it was pretty obvious that the poor, slow English were going to lose the war, and it wouldn't do to be stamped as an anglophile in the post-war academic world. He poured himself another *Doppelkorn* and began to think about the possibility — but not very seriously ...

* Head of the German Navy.

# FIVE

*"Scheisse — ver fuchte — Scheisse!" Leutnant* Dietz, the CO of the U-102, cursed, when Fritz Haberkamp, his second-in-command handed him the message. "Another *blitz?"* *

"Yes, skipper and from the Big Lion** himself."

"Today they shit on us," Dietz said and took the message closer to the light cast by a grill-covered bulb to see it better.

"Well, skipper?"

Dietz pushed his salt-encrusted white cap to the back of his blond, curly hair and grinned; "Well, Fritz." He paused, and savoured the moment. "It looks as if the Big Lion has just tossed us a nice juicy piece of meat." He gave the message to Fritz, who according to naval tradition would never read it before the captain. "Cast your big orbs on that."

Haberkamp whistled through his teeth. "Last position, estimated course — *alles!"* he exclaimed, and making all of ten knots!"

Dietz grinned. "It couldn't be much easier, could it, eh?"

"No, it couldn't, skipper."

"There'll be a piece of tin in it for you, Fritz and no doubt I'll cure my throat ache on this one." He fingered his collar as if he could already feel the Knight's Cross of the Iron Cross dangling there and curing his "throat ache". Then he was businesslike again. "All right, Fritz, let's get down the chart and work it out."

* Emergency, top priority.
** Admiral Doenitz, head of the German submarine service.]

Thus the two young men, who were already hardened, ruthless veterans, in spite of the light-hearted patter, began to work out the destruction of HMS *Rose.*

A thousand miles away, unknown to them, two other, far older men were trying to prevent just such an event taking place. But they were finding it hard going. At his end of the phone in his secret country retreat, Churchill, called hurriedly from his lunch to take Mountbatten's call, growled: "But the weather's excellent here, Mountbatten. This morning we even had a bit of sun."

"That may be, sir," Mountbatten could not quite conceal his annoyance with the Prime Minister's lack of comprehension, "but the coast and the Channel now report heavy fog. Coastal Command is fogged in."

Churchill took a hearty drink of the brandy which he had providently brought to the phone from the dining room. "Now, look here, Mountbatten. You say the *Rose* has reported her position in a code that took the DNI* no more than a few minutes to decipher —"

"Yessir."

"Well, what is there to prevent the Hun from doing the same thing?" He barked an answer to his own question before Mountbatten could reply. "Nothing — absolutely nothing! So we must get the Sunderlands up, looking for the *Rose* and giving her what protection they can. She's going to need it!"

"But sir, even if they took off against the advice of Coastal Command, how would they find the *Rose* in such a peasouper?"

"There are no buts," Churchill snapped and suddenly Mountbatten knew he was risking his career. The Prime Minister was not a man to tolerate opposition in subordinates for very long. He would sack the King's cousin as quickly as he would a less exalted person. "Those Sunderlands are laden down with costly equipment to cope with such a situation. They should be able to find the *Rose,* fog or no fog. And mind this, Mountbatten. I would rather lose a whole squadron of flying boats than one more destroyer,

* The Dept. of Naval Intelligence.

however ancient and badly damaged. The lifeblood of this country
— the convoys — flows only by virtue of the destroyers. We cannot
afford to lose a single one. Mountbatten, alert the Sunderlands!"

Abruptly the scrambler phone went dead in Mountbatten's
hand, leaving him cursing, futilely.

# SIX

"Sir."

The voice seemed to come from far, far away. Lamb kept his eyes firmly closed with determination.

*"Sir!"* Doan's voice became more insistent.

He groaned, but still did not open his eyes. It was over forty-eight hours since he had first come back on the bridge after the dawn cat-nap off St Nazaire and he was tired, unbelievably tired.

"Sir, you must wake up." Doan overstepped all naval decorum and taking hold of the captain's shoulder, shook it vigorously, as he slumped in his canvas chair on the bridge. *"SIR!"*

Lamb opened his eyes at last and stared up at Doan in the cold grey light of the new dawn, as if he were seeing him for the very first time. "What is it?" he asked suddenly, wiping the scum off his dry lips.

"The fo'c'sle, sir."

It seemed to take Lamb a long, long time to understand the simple sentence. Then he said, slowly and very carefully: "What's wrong with fo'c'sle, Doan?"

"The bow's starting to bend up again, skipper."

What?" Suddenly Lamb was wide awake, the overwhelming lethargy forgotten in an instant. "What did you say, Number One?"

"Have a look for yourself, skipper. You can see it from here. It's definitely bending up."

Hurriedly Lamb rose to his feet. Doan was right. The whole fo'c'sle was beginning to go. Soon their buoyancy would worsen,

149

the trim would go and their screws would be forced out of the water. They would be useless. "Balls", he cursed.

"Balls it is, sir." Doan answered. "Very large balls indeed."

Lamb swung round on him. "How far from land are we, Number One?"

Doan shrugged miserably. "Sixty miles or more still, sir."

"That much!"

"What are we going to do, sir?"

"We could stop altogether and wait for somebody to find us," Lamb said and giggled absurdly like a schoolboy, overcome by the absolute, almost unbearable strain of the last two days. "It's April Fool's Day, isn't it?" Hurriedly he pulled himself together, his thin grey face with the heavy bags under the eyes, normal again. "Or we could reduce speed again and take our chance with the U-boats. This damned fog must lift soon. Then the Sunderlands will find us, or what's left of us." He tried to smile to cheer Doan up, but failed miserably. A minute later, HMS *Rose* was limping along at exactly one and half knots. Now she was a perfect target for any lurking German submarine.


An hour later, the problem of submarines was forgotten completely, although Lamb had every man off-watch on deck as look-out. Now his only concern was the forward bulkhead. Even at a speed of one and half knots, the bow of the ship was beginning to sink lower and lower into the water and from below an appalling knocking, of protesting metal strained to its absolute limit could be heard. As Wide Boy said to Scouse, all his usual bravado gone now, "It sounds as if the old bitch is ripe for the knacker's yard!" And all that Scouse, as pale as his younger companion, could summon up by way of a reply was: "Ay, yer right there, mate."

By noon that first of April, 1942, in England, in another world, *"Workers" Playtime* was in full swing, housewives were preparing the Monday stew, and trade unionists were nodding their heads sagely at the *Daily Mirror's* latest cartoon, which showed a shipwrecked sailor on a raft in the middle of nowhere above a caption which read *The Price of Petrol has been increased by a penny — official"*.

And by noon, the *Rose* had come to a virtual stop as she faced into the wind.

Lamb dared not give her the rudder leverage, which an increase in speed would have afforded. As a result she lay in the wave troughs, tumbled back and forth by the waves, barely responding to the helm. Leading Seaman Callaghan, who was at the wheel, whispered to Degenhardt, "Chief, it's no bloody good." He sighed with weary fatalism. "The *Rose* ain't answering anymore."

Degenhardt, as weary as the rest of them, turned slowly to the big seaman, whose father, he knew had once been a chief himself. It took the wizened CPO a long time to find the words he sought, and when they came out, they were harsh, determined and brutal. "Well if you don't believe in the *Rose,* you long streak of Pompey piss, get off the fucking helm!" He shoved by the big sailor and seized the wheel himself. Callaghan began to sob.


The hands had about had it, Lamb could see that. The eyes of those on watch were red and strained and they had to lean against the bulkheads for support. When cooks brought them up the inevitable stale corned beef sandwiches, they could scarcely move their jaws to bite into the bread. Twice, Degenhardt, who was accompanying Lamb on his tour of the deck, had to bark at a weary hand, who was sleeping standing up at his post, eyes closed.

"They're buggered, sir," Degenhardt said slowly, as if even the iron CPO could hardly summon up enough strength to form a coherent sentence.

"Yes, I know," Lamb replied simply. He peered desperately through the grey, sad, dripping mist, willing himself to see the land that meant so much, but seeing nothing but sea and fog. Yet like a man in delirium, light-headed and unrealistic, he would not give up. They must soon see land. The *Rose* demanded they should. He turned to Degenhardt. "Issue more rum," he ordered in a cracked voice. "They have to keep going."

"Sir," Degenhardt said automatically, and looked at the Captain, his face shocked.

"Scouse," the Wide Boy croaked, his thirst not helped by the tot of rum for very long, "I'm out on me feet. I've had it."

"You'll have the toe of me boot up yer arse, if you dare close yer sodding eyes," Scouse snarled and rubbed his weary, red-rimmed eyes with his knuckles: "You're on look-out, remember and they can shoot you if yer kip."

"Let them," Wide Boy answered through lips which were white with scum. "It'd be a relief. Then I could get a bit o' shut-eye."

Scouse caught him by the arm and pushed him against the Lewis gun's butt — hard. Wide Boy yelped with the sudden pain. "What did yer go and do that for?"

"Because you're not kipping on this post, you Cockney clot! That's why. Yer in the Royal Navy, lad, and we don't do things like that." He rammed Wide Boy against the gun butt again. "Now open them eyes!"

Wide Boy did as he was ordered, and Scouse breathed out hard, as if he'd run an exhausting long race.

The afternoon passed leadenly. The look-out men staggered like drunks as they walked their stretch of deck, peering out through half-closed eyes at the endless, swaying green swathe of sea. Nothing!

Whatever the direction, the result was always the same — nothing. The sea was devoid of everything. For all they knew, the rest of the world might have been destroyed by some gigantic bomb, leaving them — unknowing — in their heaving, swaying, groaning piece of wrecked metal, the only ones still alive.

On the bridge, listening to the appalling racket from the fo'c'sle, Lamb viewed the sea with lack-lustre eyes and wondered whether, in the end, it was worth it. Were they perhaps all going to perish after all? Might it not be that next big wave would swamp the fo'c'sle, rip the last of the patch away and take them to the bottom of the sea to become yet another of those countless mysteries of the sea, which would intrigue newspaper readers one morning — "the admiralty regrets to announce that the HMS *Rose*" — for a few moments, and then be forgotten for all time?

Inside him his own weary voice urged him on: "Of course, it's worth it! You must keep going. *You must!*"

Lamb nodded his agreement, his eyes wild with fatigue. He must keep a grip on himself — and his crew. Probably he'd had less sleep than anyone else on board the *Rose,* but still he was responsible for the lot of them. He had to keep going. In a broken, cracked voice, he cried to Degenhardt, who was still at the wheel after taking over from Callaghan, who had collapsed below in a state of shock: "Chief, keep the bloody ship on course, can't you!"

Degenhardt said nothing, as he fought to keep the rolling, bumping *Rose* on some semblance of a course, but he knew in his heart that the end was near now.


Thus HMS *Rose* staggered on, taking more and more water, fighting back with determination, but losing all the time. Her bow sank lower and lower. The noise from the fo'c'sle had now reached an ear-splitting shrill peak, as if she might fall apart at any moment. But gallant and brave to the very end, she refused to give up, rolling ever further northwards towards the land that stubbornly refused to reveal itself.

# SEVEN

"Object — green, one zero, sir!" Haberkamp shouted, the wind tearing the words from his mouth, as the two of them crouched in the bitter cold of the open conning tower.

Dietz swung his big binoculars round speedily.

The U-102 dipped suddenly and reared up again; then he saw it — a brief glimpse of wrecked superstructure and the white of the ensign, hanging limply at her bow. Next to him, Haberkamp was already leafing hurriedly through the recognition tables.

"Well?" he snapped, very professional now.

"Yes skipper. *Flower* class, 1918. Only one constructed under the British Admiralty's Emergency War Programme."

"Then it's the *Rose* all right."

"Right, skipper."

The two young officers flung up their glasses again and caught the destroyer once more as the U-102 rose on the swell. "She's taken a bad beating, Fritz," Dietz said, noting the terribly crumpled bow with satisfaction. "And she must be making all of two knots. Forward gun turret's gone too."

"You're right, sir." The First Officer swung his glasses the length of the ship. "Her depth charges are intact and the rear gun turret."

"Yes, I've already noted that," Dietz broke in, his mind now beginning to race, as he considered the best way of attack. "How far are we from the English coast?" Dietz asked suddenly.

"About forty sea miles, sir."

"I see." Dietz lowered his glasses and thought. As soon as the U-102 attacked, the British would naturally be squawking for help to their air force and it wouldn't take them long to be on the scene, especially now the fog was beginning to lift. In short, his attack would have to be swift and decisive. He made his decision.

"Fritz, we shall make a surface attack," he announced.

"But they've got their guns aft still, sir."

"I know. But I want to make sure. In this damn fog we'll be able to get damn close without their spotting us. We'll let her have tubes one to four midships and then crash dive. It'll be as easy as getting it inside one of those plump, knowing little schoolgirls you pick up on the Jungfernstieg* when you're on leave." He grinned and Haberkamp grinned back. The skipper was always pulling his leg about the high school girls on whom his elegant blue naval uniform seemed to work like an aphrodisiac.

"All right," Dietz raised his voice above the roar of the waves, "action stations everywhere. We're going into the attack!"


Moodily Scouse was crooning one of his own compositions, to the tune of the *Lincolnshire Poacher,* as he and Wide Boy crouched next to the Lewis Gun, their red-rimmed eyes narrowed to slits against the wind: *That Hitler's armies can beat us, is just a lot of cock. Marshal Timoshenko's boys are pissing through von Bock. The Führer makes the bloomers and his marshals take the rap. Meanwhile Joe smokes his pipe and wears a taxi-driver's cap.*

"Blimey, can't yer put a sock in it, Scouse?" Wide Boy groaned, his cracked voice heavy with weariness. "Yer've been singing that sodding thing the last sodding hour or more."

"You ain't got no ear for music, you ain't," Scouse replied without rancour. "Besides it's a bit of a song of praise for our allies, the Russkies. They're doing the real fighting, yer know."

Wide Boy sighed. "And what do yer think we're sodding well doing out here in the middle of the drink — sodding well knitting!"

* Fashionable street in Hamburg.

"Ner, but I mean it stands to reason, don't it. We're doing our bit here —" He stopped abruptly. "What's that over there?" he snapped, his voice suddenly very hard, all tiredness gone now.

"What's what?"

"There over to port! Long black object." Scouse capped his hands to his mouth and yelled desperately at the top of his voice. "Sir ... sir! *Jerry sub off the port bow!*" With one vicious jab of his elbow, he thrust Wide Boy out of the way and grasping the butt of the Lewis gun, snapped off the safety catch, as all over the stricken *Rose,* the alarm bells began to sound their urgent, frightening warning.

On the conning-tower, Dietz, his bearded face set and hard, watched the crippled British destroyer grow ever larger in his glasses. Down below, every man was at his station in the yellow depressing light, faces tense and greasy with sweat, ready for his command.

"Six thousand metres!" Haberkamp crouched over the range finder called out.

Dietz did not react. They were still not close enough to their unsuspecting victim. They must hit her the first time and then disappear beneath the heaving green waves before the RAF appeared.

"Five thousand metres!" Haberkamp yelled five minutes later. "Target Green 90! Speed two knots!"

Dietz gnawed his bottom lip, knowing that the others on the conning-tower could not see his gesture of indecision. In the forced intimacy of a submarine, a captain must never reveal his doubts to the crew; it would destroy their confidence in him. Still he wondered whether or not he was not chancing his luck a little too far. The *Rose* would spot him soon; she *had* to. Yet all the same he must be sure of his kill.

"All lined up!" the torpedo petty officer's voice came up from below. Dietz could visualize him bent over the attack table, connected as it was with the gyro-compass and attack sight, transmitting the firing settings to the torpedoes, which would be reproduced in the set of their angling mechanism. The long grey deadly fish with their two tons of high explosive were ready to go.

"Ready!" Dietz snapped suddenly, speaking for the first time since they had begun their attack approach.

"Ready, captain!" the petty officer snapped back.

"Thank you, Petty Officer. Prepare to fire!" Now all banter had gone from his voice, as he stood on the wildly heaving conning-tower like a grim Nordic god, moisture dripping from his leather suit, and opaque pearls of spume hanging in his beard and eyebrows, ready to give the order that would send the ancient British destroyer plunging to the depths. He took a deep breath and opened his mouth to pronounce the *Rose's* death sentence. Just at that moment the red and white tracer came zigzagging flatly over the water towards him, gathering tremendous speed the closer it got. Five hundred metres away the sea was ripped apart by the Lewis gun's bullets falling far short of the German submarine.

*Leutnant zur See* Dietz hesitated for just one moment. But it was a moment too long. To the aft of the almost stationary destroyer, a brazen light broke the greyness of the afternoon. There was a horrid frightening sound like a great piece of canvas being ripped apart. And a second later, the huge hollow echoing whack of metal striking metal. X-turret's shell exploded just in front of the conning-tower, and in the scarlet flare of angry flame, Dietz glimpsed Haberkamp flying crazily through the air — minus his arms and head — as the explosion threw him to the deck.


*"Torpedoes!"* Doan gasped frantically. "Degenhardt —"

"Seen them, sir!" Degenhardt yelled and flung the wheel hard over to starboard, as the long trails of crazy white bubbles flashed closer and closer.

"Chief, give it all —" Lamb's words froze on his lips. There was no more he could say. Everything lay in Degenhardt's hands and the *Rose's* response.

They waited. The *Rose* seemed to take an incredibly long time to answer to the helm: The crazy white trails grew ever closer. Lamb dug his nails cruelly into the sweaty palms of his hands.

Would she make it? Then shaking horribly, the noise in her fo'c'sle rising to a banshee wail, she began to come round. They had perhaps ten seconds left. Out of the corner of his eye, Lamb, the sweat pouring off his body in spite of the bitter cold, could see the wide, white V of the four torpedoes' wakes, as they homed in on the *Rose*. *Five seconds!* The whole ship was shaking madly now, as if she might fall apart at any moment. *Three seconds:* Aft, X-turret was pounding away crazily at the submarine, aided by MacFadden's Lewis gun. In one second, all that frenetic chatter would be silenced for good, if —

Abruptly the torpedoes were flashing by harmlessly to starboard, and *Rose* was still miraculously alive! But the torpedoes would run on until their motors gave out, and they would sink to the bottom of the Channel to be dredged out, rusty, encrusted, fossilized in another age to be wondered at and puzzled about, as evidence of a time that no one could quite understand.

"Oh, *brother!*" Doan gasped and leaned limply against the bridge.

"Good show, exceedingly good show, Degenhardt!" Lamb cried in a passable imitation of how a regular Royal Navy officer should behave at such a moment, though he had never, in his whole life, felt less like playing a role — his hands were trembling violently. "You certainly saved our bacon then."

"*I* didn't sir." Degenhardt yelled back above the roar of X-turret. "It was the *Rose,* sir. She answered to the helm as if she were a two-year old, not a raddled old bitch ten times that age! She just won't give up ..."


"*Stand fast, everybody!*" Dietz yelled urgently, as the yellow cloud of acrid fumes vanished and he could see that the conning-tower had been very badly hit — too much so for them to submerge safely now. He staggered across the bloody mess in the bottom of the tower, which had once been the look-out, and kicked Haberkamp's head out of the way. "All right down there?" he cried down the ladder into the submarine's interior.

"All right, sir!" someone called back. Just a couple of casualties."

"Good. But the boat —" Dietz caught himself in time. They need not know yet that they could no longer submerge.

"Gun crew on deck — at the double. Bow tubes — three and four — stand by for surface fire."

There was a clatter of heavy, nailed sea boots on the dripping iron ladder. Bearded, pale-faced young men in leather clothing pushed by the captain and dropping over the side of the shattered conning tower, doubled across the narrow curving deck. Another rating swung himself behind the twin Spandau on the tower itself and with hardly a second's hesitation, began pouring a stream of tracer at the destroyer, only a couple of thousand metres away, while the gun crew fumbled frantically with the slick tarpaulin which covered the bow gun. Across the water the British worked on their own guns, ready to fire again.

Dietz looked at the conning tower and cursed again. "Those shitty bastards," he cried to himself and promising that he would sink the destroyer come what may. The British would suffer for what they had just done to the U-102.

"Almost ready, sir!" the torpedo petty officer yelled.

The boat lurched noticeably. That would be the engineers, Dietz told himself, already beginning to flood the tanks to compensate for the loss of the torpedoes' weight. Now their hands would be itchy on the controls, ready to take the U-102 down in a crash dive. Dietz knew he should warn them that this was no longer possible but his mind was full of revenge. First, he must sink the *Rose.*

"Stand by to fire!" he commanded.


"What now, skipper?" Doan cried in alarm above the thud-thud of "X" turret and the wild chatter of the Lewis gun.

Lamb took in the situation in a flash. "She's been badly hit in the conning tower and she's broadsides on to us. At that angle she'll have to do some pretty nice deflection shooting with those torpedoes of hers if she's going to hit us."

Doan's heart raced with new hope. Of course! The Kraut sub. would have to fire its fish at an angle of 45°. At the firing control, they would be aiming due north, while looking northeast. "All the same, they *could* pull it off."

"Agreed," Lamb said, keeping his eyes glued on the submarine, with the dark shapes of the gunners scrambling down the buckled conning tower ladder and pelting for the deck gun. "But we're not going to help them ... Degenhardt as soon as I yell "Now", swing her round to port!"

"Ay, ay, sir," Degenhardt answered promptly and gripped the wheel in his brown claws, as if he were prepared to turn the *Rose* by brute force when the time came.

"You see, Doan," Lamb explained hastily. "At this range, we might have ten to twelve seconds between the time the Jerry fires and the time the torpedoes reach us. With a bit of luck, if we spot them as soon as they leave the sub the *Rose 'll* answer straight away and come round."

With a *lot* of luck, skipper," Doan rapped and then realized immediately that he should have bitten back the words, for in the Captain's eyes the *Rose* would never let them down. On the bridge the tension was electric. Everything now depended on the battered, hard-pressed old destroyer.


*"Come on ... come on ... get on with yer!"* Scouse cursed to himself as he fumbled with the new pan of ammunition he was fitting to the smoking, glowing Lewis gun. He slapped the drum with the flat of his hand, his eyes fixed on the German gunners swinging their cannon round to bear on the *Rose,* to assure himself that it was securely fixed and yelled. "On!"

"Ta!" Wide Boy cried and tucked the machine gun's wooden butt into his shoulder. Aft of the *Rose,* the "X" turret's twin 5 inchers were concentrating desperately on the sub's turret. Instinctively he swung the Lewis gun to the U-boat's deck cannon. "All right, you Jerry buggers, let's see yer started on the two-step!" he grunted and pulled the trigger.

The butt thudded against his shoulder, as the ancient World War I machine gun chattered into violent life. Tracer zipped across the water. A man bringing up a shell on the U-boat's deck was hit. He dropped his burden, his hands flying upwards, outstretched fingers fanning the air wildly, like a dancer in the black minstrel shows that Wide Boy had enjoyed as a kid.

"Got him!" Scouse cried in delight. "Got him, you jammy bugger!"

Wide Boy grinned at the praise and swung the gun round towards the men fumbling with the Jerry gun. His burst caught two Germans slightly to the right of it. They were swatted over the side of the submarine like flies.

"That's the ticket, lad," Scouse yelled, besides himself with joy. "That's the stuff to give the troops —"

He never finished the sentence. The German gun cracked into action with a thick, frightening crump. A flash of violent, yellow flame. The shell whistled shrilly across the thousand yards of water separating the two almost stationary ships and exploded directly to their front. Scouse felt himself lifted high in the air and slammed by the great blast against the deck; then a huge roaring red-blackness overcame him and he lost consciousness, at that same moment a fatally wounded Wide Boy started to crawl back to the still intact gun on his bleeding hands and knees, his dying eyes full of only one desire — to kill ...

"ON!" the torpedo petty officer screamed above the clash of the battle over his head.

Dietz hesitated no longer. "FIRE!" he yelled.

The submarine lurched once. Their first fish had been launched. Automatically Dietz waited another one and one-fifth seconds. The U-102 shuddered again. Their second torpedo was underway.

Hurriedly he flung up his glasses, ignoring the Tommy gun which was firing away at regular intervals, but with little effect. Below, the torpedo petty officer was counting off aloud the seconds till the fish struck. On the conning tower, Dietz watched them

161

running through the water, their sharp white tail trailing behind them like the wake of a vicious shark. He clutched his glasses savagely, feeling the sweat trickling down the small of his back. The tension was almost unbearable. They must hit the *Rose* this time before fleeing on the surface to the cover of the nearest French port. *They had to!*

*"NOW!"* Lamb screamed, letting his binoculars drop to his heaving chest.

Degenhardt acted at once. He flung his whole weight against the wheel, the purple veins standing out on his brown, wrinkled temples.

Lamb and Doan waited, bodies already tensed for that tremendous roar and shattering explosion which would mean the end.

Nothing happened! The *Rose* seemed as if she had given up at last, and no longer had the will to fight; as if she were prepared to accept her terrible fate. Lamb dug his nails cruelly into the palms of his hands. *Would she never move?*

*"Beweg' dich, du Sau!"* Degenhardt cursed savagely, forgetting his mother's tongue and using the one he had once sworn he would never speak again. He asserted even wilder pressure.

Off their battered side, the torpedo trails were getting closer and closer. It could only be a matter of seconds now.

Slowly the *Rose* began to turn. The compass trembled. A point ... Another point. She was turning — very definitely turning. Lamb, his face as white as the compass-card, ran to the side of the bridge.

"Torpedo — port bow!" someone screamed hysterically. Lamb did not hear. His eyes were fixed on that white hissing wake. And then the first one was passed in a straight, arrow-headed line, with inches to spare. An instant later and the second one was on them. Lamb prayed desperately that it would be to the off-side of the first one. But his prayer was not answered.

With a paralysed feeling of uncontrollable horror, he heard the hollow boom of steel striking steel, and clenched his fists frantically ready for the explosion. The *Rose* had failed. She had been hit.

The silence continued. Nothing happened. The ship went on making her infinitely slow and weary circle to port. The torpedo had failed to explode! And suddenly both Lamb and Degenhardt were shouting at each other crazily and yelling with laughter and Doan, clutching the bridge, said weakly, "Oh Jesus, I think I just wet my skivvies! ..."

# EIGHT

*"Both engines — ahead!"* Dietz screamed.

The U-102 leapt forward. At the gun, the crew were firing full out. On the conning-tower, the twin Spandau joined in, an instant later, as the submarine swung round, churning an arc of wild water behind her, and headed straight for the crippled British destroyer.

The *Rose* fired back desperately. A shell glanced off the U-102's bow. She reeled wildly and a hole appeared in the tough Krupp steel. Shrapnel scythed through the air and pattered on the deck like heavy rain. One of the gun crew screamed and went overboard to disappear in the submarine's turbulent wake.

"Help ... help me!" he cried frantically.

Deitz did not turn his head. Now he was concerned with one thing only — the destruction of that damned monster which had almost crippled his beautiful 102. He would sink her, if it were the last thing he ever did in his short life.

Now he could make out every detail of his opponent — from the white blobs of the crew's faces, as they pelted along the destroyer's deck, to her screws almost raised out of the water, gleaming and steely-bright in comparison to the rusty green of the barnacles beyond. She was his for the taking now. He would ram her in the bows where she was already almost under water, shear them off — or at least seal her fate by enlarging the huge ragged hole there — and then head for home, leaving her to sink in her own time. But sink her he would.

An enemy shell exploded at the deck gun. The gunners reeled back in all directions, their violently twisting bodies running scarlet. Red-hot slivers of gleaming metal hissed through the air. At his side the Spandau gunner screamed shrilly and clasped a frantic hand to his shoulder, where the blood was already beginning to jet out in a cascade.

Dietz did not even notice. "More speed," he commanded recklessly. "Give me more damn speed, will you!"

Below, the frightened, ashen-faced engine-room artificer looked up at the skipper's distorted, wild-eyed features and knew that he was mad.

"He's going to ram us, skipper!" Doan yelled in alarm, as the submarine grew ever larger, an angry white bone of water at her holed bow. "The crazy bastard's going to smash into us!"

Lamb looked at the U-boat, her deck littered with the dead gun crew, desperately. Doan was right. But there was nothing he could do about it. The *Rose* was too far gone to manoeuvre any more.

"X-turret," he yelled, hands clasped around his mouth, "knock the bugger out — knock the bugger, out, can't you!"

But even as he said the words, he knew they were useless. If the sweating, black-grimed gunners *could* have heard him, they could still not have stopped the narrow submarine hurtling hull-down towards them. That would have required a shot in a million. And X-turret did not have that kind of gunner in its crew.

Yet someone heard Captain Lamb. Vaguely, the voice echoing back and forth in the chambers of his mind, as if heard from far, far below the water, the dying Wide Boy heard it. He blinked his eyes rapidly several times. Nothing focused. Then, as if in a dream, he became aware of the Lewis gun's wooden, blood-drenched butt just in front of his eyes, waving back and forth in the red mist, which threatened to submerge him at any moment.

*"Knock her out .... for God's sake ... "* the familiar voice, he could no longer place, penetrated into his consciousness. "Ay, ay, sir," he mumbled and lifted the butt.

Through the trembling ring sight he saw the monstrous grey shape hurtling towards them with the streaming white and black flag showing its crooked cross, and high up, as if floating on the water, the pale blur of a face. Instinctively he knew it must be that of the Jerry captain. With the last of his strength, he pressed the trigger. The gun burst in one final hectic moment of life, then the blood flooded Wide Boy's throat as he slumped over the butt. Harmlessly, the gun chattered to a stop, pointing straight upwards into the grey sky, which was now loud with the noise of the Sunderlands' motors. Wide Boy Stevens would never see that brave new world and "the loot, the mazuma, the lolly" — the pickings — which he had thought were so important for happiness. For now he was dead.

That final burst ripped open *Leutnant zur See* Dietz's chest and flung him down the ladder into a crumpled, dead heap at its base.

*"Dive ... dive ... dive!"* the engineer screamed, as the helmsman swung the U-102 off its collision course, and the klaxons started to sound their urgent warning.

But it was already too late!

The heavy-bellied, four-engined, white-painted Sunderlands had come roaring in from the west completely unobserved. Now the three of them came winging in low, the doors in their bellies wide-open. The bombs began tumbling out of them, revolving over and over, as they headed straight for their target.

The first hundred pounder caught the U-102 aft. She shuddered violently. The jack and its crooked-cross flag vanished in a thick burst of flame and smoke. Down below, the lights went out and suddenly there were screams of fear, angry cries, yelps of pain everywhere, as the cold sea water started to pour in mercilessly through the buckled steel plates.

But the pilots of the four-engined Coastal Command planes knew no remorse. They hated these lean, grey sea-wolves, who had brought England to the verge of starvation. They came in again, as the survivors, screaming with panic, clawing and fighting each other in their desperation to escape, clambered up from the shambles below and started throwing themselves over the side, already thick with escaping oil.

A bomb hit the U-102 amidships. She shuddered wildly. She was hit again. Thick black smoke started to pour from her open conning tower. Below, her diesel ignited. Five hundred yards away, the open-mouthed, awe-struck spectators on the *Rose* felt the shock like searing wet heat striking them across the face. Scarlet flame leapt up, high in the air. In the water, already alight themselves, the handful of survivors struck out desperately to escape the funeral pyre. In vain. One by one they were overtaken by the flames and consumed by them. The Sunderlands, heavy, majestic, in full control of the situation, now came in for one last run. A final bomb struck the burning submarine on her bow. It was all was needed to finish her off. Almost casually she rolled over like a dead whale, exposed her ugly, red-painted belly, and with one last flurry of white water, slipped beneath the waves and was gone for ever ...

The trio of Sunderlands came in low, wagging their wings ponderously in a heavy-bellied imitation of a fighter signalling a victory.

Below, the crew of the *Rose,* hardly believing that they had been saved after all, raised a hoarse cheer for them. Slowly one of the Coastal Command planes — probably the flight leader — peeled off and came down very low in a slow curve, its propellers feathered back almost to stalling speed.

A signal lamp began to flicker off and on in its cabin. "Yeoman!" Lamb barked. "Read him please."

Leading Signalman Smith, Scouse's mate Bunts, wiped the little Liverpudlian's blood off his hands and started spelling out the message. *"Having a spot of bother ... down there, Navy ...; need any help to get you back to Falmouth? ... Over to you"*

Lamb hesitated for an instant, but only for an instant "Send him this, Yeoman." He ordered.

"Sir."

*"Help? ... not Pygmalion likely! HMS Rose will make own way."*

Bunts looked at him in astonishment. "Beg pardon, sir?"

"Just send it, Bunts," Lamb ordered grinning. "It's just a quote that's all."

"Ay, ay, sir," Bunts said and bent over the Aldis lamp; officers and gentlemen were funny buggers at the best of times ...

# Epilogue

"Well, MacFadden you rogue, how are you feeling?" Commander Lamb kept his voice low, aware of the crowded sick bay, with its groaning wounded and those who no longer groaned, but stared straight ahead with eyes that knew no light.

"Not so hot, sir," Scouse whispered through the bandages, which wreathed his head. "But never say die."

"Yes, that's the spirit, never say die," Lamb answered.

"How's the Wide Boy, beg pardon, sir, Able Seaman Stevens?"

Lamb hesitated only for a fraction of a second. "I'm afraid he's dead, MacFadden. He did a very brave thing. He stuck to his post, severely wounded, firing his weapon till the end came. If there were enough gongs to go round, I'd recommend him for one."

MacFadden nodded his head painfully. "Thought he had it in him. His dad got a gong in the last lot, sir. Said it was a load of balls, but I knew when the chips was down, he'd come through trumps."

Lamb nodded silently. "Now you get some shut-eye, MacFadden. The jab should start working any moment now."

"Thank you, sir." Scouse looked up suddenly at the captain, eyes already hazy with pain and drugs. "Do you think it was all worth it, sir?" he asked, completely out of the blue.

"Worth what?" Lamb asked in surprise.

"This little lot." Weakly MacFadden indicated the suffering all around him in the sick bay.

"Of course —" Lamb stopped abruptly, as the full impact of the question hit him. Who would remember St Nazaire and those desperate hours off the coast of France in twenty years' time, or even ten? Who would remember Wall-Jones' desperate charge; the way Leading Seaman Callaghan broke down, how Wide Boy Stevens manned the Lewis to the end and all the rest of it? *Who!* He pulled himself together. "Of course it was all worth it, MacFadden. Hasn't it helped to win the war and isn't that the most important thing in the world for us?"

But MacFadden's head had already tilted to one side, his eyes closed, his breathing harsh and loud in his drugged sleep. Lamb shrugged and passed on through the line of stretchers to where Doan had suddenly appeared for him at the door of the sick bay.

"What is it, Number One?" he whispered urgently. "And what the devil are you grinning like a damned Cheshire cat for?"

"Come and have a look topside, sir. We're about to enter Falmouth harbour!"


It was a beautiful morning. The rays of the spring sun fell warmly on the harbour, turning the little white houses around the blue bay, pale pink, and waving shadows across the hills in the far distance. Lamb turned his pale, unshaven young face to the sun's rays for an instant and then winked triumphantly at Doan. "The old *Rose* made it after all, didn't she, Number One!"

"She sure did, sir." Doan responded enthusiastically.

Lamb's grin vanished. "Well?" he demanded.

"Well, what sir?" Doan asked puzzled.

"Harbour stations — that's what, Number One. We're a warship, so we should have harbour stations."

"Ay, ay, sir!" Doan snapped back. He would never understand the English if he lived to be a hundred. Harbour stations on a beat-up old heap of scrap-iron like this, which couldn't make more than two knots!

Behind him Chief Petty Officer Degenhardt grinned cautiously.

Slowly HMS *Rose* began to edge her way painfully towards the entrance, while Lamb himself took the bridge. "Take a signal, yeoman," he snapped, as they approached the boom.

"Sir," Bunts answered, poised at the Aldis.

"To Port War Signal Station, Falmouth, to pass on to Flag Officer, Falmouth. His Majesty's Ship *Rose* will enter harbour at approximately eight hundred hours. Ship — er," Lamb cleared his throat, as if suddenly embarrassed — "somewhat damaged. Request assistance of tug. Please have medical attention waiting. We have casualties." He resumed briskly. "All clear, Smith?"

"Ay, ay, sir." Bunts answered promptly and began flicking his lamp rapidly.

Minutes later the boom was going up and they were limping into the harbour, crowded with the usual ships of an ordinary day in spring in the middle of the war. Yet there was nothing usual about the behaviour of the men on those ships, naval and merchant seamen; for they were cheering the battered ship and from over at the dockside, the factory sirens were beginning to join in until the whole harbour seemed to be one shrill, frantic, all-consuming cry of joyous acclaim and welcome.

Lamb shook his head forcibly to clear away the blur in front of his eyes and punched the bulkhead hard. *"Bugger you Rose,"* he whispered to no one in particular, *"you've done it again ..."*

THE END

**If you enjoyed this book, look for others like it at Thunderchild Publishing: https://ourworlds.net/thunderchild_cms/**

Made in the USA
Las Vegas, NV
21 May 2022

49189346R00095